Language Lessons

By the Author

All This Time

The Meaning of Liberty

Language Lessons

As Jordan Meadows:

Proximity

Not Just Friends

Language Lessons

by

Sage Donnell

2024

LANGUAGE LESSONS

ISBN 13: 978-1-63679-725-0

This Trade Paperback Original Is Published By
Bold Strokes Books, Inc.
P.O. Box 249
Valley Falls, NY 12185

First Edition: October 2024

Credits
Editor: Barbara Ann Wright
Production Design: Susan Ramundo
Cover Design By Tammy Seidick

Acknowledgments

I'd like to thank the entire Bold Strokes team for putting my books out into the world.

Haley, this book has many of your fingerprints on it from inspiring the playful nature of this one to me being blown away by your language skills. So, a particular thank you for all of that, but also for giving me access to native Czech speakers. That was a huge help.

Thanks, also, to Alison, Anthony, Lia, and Mom for always supporting my writing dreams.

Dedication

As always to my daughter, Haley.
Without you, there'd be no books.

Chapter One

"I believe clothing should be optional in the home."

It was all Grace could do not to put her face in her hands. The eighty-bajillionth roommate candidate had been promising up until they said that. Grace wouldn't judge the general concept. People could do what they wanted in the privacy of their own homes but not in the privacy of her home. She was not that comfortable with nudity, particularly the nudity of a man she'd known all of ten minutes. It was problematic from both the man and the practical stranger viewpoint. "I'm not comfortable with that."

"You should really open up your mind."

And now he was mansplaining to her? No. She was done. "Well, thanks for meeting with me, but I don't think this will work out."

"Oh, come on. We can be naked together." The last was called out to her retreating back.

Grace had interviewed her first couple of candidates in her house, thinking it would be easiest to show them the space as they interviewed. However, after having trouble getting one woman to leave, she'd switched tactics. She now met them in coffee shops where she could be the one to leave. She wanted to do that now, but she had a desperate need to pee, so she walked to the back to use the restroom. She only hoped he'd be gone when she came back out.

He wasn't. Grace ducked back into the hall leading to the bathroom to figure out her next move. She could walk out. The worst that would happen was that he'd yell something else at her.

But that was unpleasant, and she wanted to avoid it if possible. To kill time, she perused the community bulletin board. This wasn't her usual coffee shop. She didn't want to contaminate that one with the unpleasant interviews.

There were performances advertised, offers of pet sitting and child tutoring, and one that asked if you had a spare room in your home. Grace zeroed in on that. It was an organization called Overseas Stays, and it was for exchange students. Students were arriving in just over two weeks, and homes were still needed. Grace checked the post date. Just yesterday. They offered money for room and board. It was a little bit more than she was asking for rent. She had to include food for the student, but maybe this was the way to go. She could lay out rules for them to follow. She worked long days, but the notice said that the students would have school and activities, so that probably wasn't a problem.

She took a picture and walked out.

"So when can I move in?" the man called as she passed.

Grace ignored him. On the sidewalk, she dialed her best friend.

"How'd it go?" Maci asked.

"Horribly. I don't know why you have to go live in romantic bliss with your boyfriend when I need a roommate." She was joking. Mostly.

"I know. I'm a scumbag." Maci sounded perfectly cheerful about it. "Was it really that bad?"

"Aside from the woman who just wouldn't leave, the worst. This guy said that we should get naked together."

"He didn't!"

"He did."

"Maybe next time, I should come with you. You know, for protection."

The idea that tiny little Maci could offer protection was laughable. She had to call Grace to help move patients in the emergency department at the hospital. Grace held back her initial reaction by pressing her lips together before saying, "It's why we're meeting in public now. It's fine. But guess what I found while I was hiding in the hall to the bathroom?"

"I don't think I want to guess."

"No, it's not bad. I found a flier for a homestay for students thing. You host an exchange student, and they give you a stipend for room and board. It's not bad, either."

"Do you really want a teenager living with you?"

"I mean, it's not ideal, but at least I get to lay down the rules. I'm getting desperate, Maci."

"I know. I'm truly sorry."

"I know you are, but I've gotta get some help with the mortgage." Grace had bought a house using down payment money she'd inherited from her grandmother, who'd stipulated it had to be used for just that. When Grace thought Maci was going to move in with her and help with the mortgage so Grace could still cover her student loan payments, that had been annoying but fine. Now, she was starting to wonder if she'd have to sell the house she'd just bought, losing a ton of money on the Realtor's cut and rent a room herself. Her finances were bleak.

"Okay, so let's talk rules. I think the first is that quiet time is between ten and six."

One of the previous candidates had asked about soundproofing because she liked to practice drums late at night. With Grace's shift at the hospital starting at seven a.m.—and not wanting to alienate her neighbors—that was a huge no. "Do you think I have to actually say no walking through the house naked, or will that get me arrested?"

"I think most teenagers aren't going to be interested in public nudity. You're probably safe to leave that off."

"Cool, cool. I think I should say no sleeping on the couch, though. I mean, there was that one person who told me they didn't need a bedroom because they preferred to sleep on the couch. Which, just no."

"Immediately a no," Maci agreed. "Do you need a rule about when windows can be open or not?"

"Um…"

"It's just that, now that I'm living with Greg, I've realized he has some bad window habits."

"Like what?" Grace stopped at an intersection and nodded at the old woman standing next to her. The woman turned away, looking annoyed. Was it from the nod or the fact that Grace was on the phone? It didn't matter, but she still felt a little bad. She took a step away to give the woman more space.

"Like having the AC on and the window open for fresh air. I was all, 'Are we solving global warming by using our AC to cool the planet? I don't think that'll work, Greg.' And he was all, 'Fresh air is good for you.' So."

"Noted. Okay, no windows open if the AC or the heat is on, I suppose." The light changed, and Grace crossed, then turned right. She was about a ten minute walk from her new house. She'd only moved into the neighborhood a month ago, and it still felt new, but generally, she loved it. Her apartment had been in a walkable neighborhood, too, and she'd been a little worried about the change. It turned out that she loved living near Alberta even more than she'd loved living near Hawthorne. Maybe it was just the freshness, and it would wear off.

They spent the rest of the walk discussing rules, cracking themselves up with going more and more esoteric. Grace was just about to turn up her walk when Maci said, "I've gotta run. I've got a dentist appointment in thirty, and I've gotta brush my teeth before I go."

"Yes, don't gross out the dentist, please. Or the hygienist."

"Let me know how it goes when you call about getting an exchange kid. A mother. At your age. Wild."

"Listen, I wasn't prepared for a teenager at twenty-five, but needs must."

It was too bad that Grace didn't have Maci on the phone to distract her from her overgrown yard as she passed through. One of the reasons she'd gotten a deal on this house was because the yard was a shambles. She'd done nothing to correct that as of yet. She didn't know what to do with a yard. She'd never had one before. Even as a kid, she and her mom had lived in an apartment. Eventually, she'd have to figure it out.

The porch, which she climbed five stairs to reach, was one of her very favorite things, even though it overlooked the messy yard. It also overlooked Holman, which was fun because it was a bike boulevard. Grace was more of a walking and driving girl, but she liked watching the bikes go by.

She opened her door, and Loki tore out. She'd tried to keep the little tortoiseshell cat inside when they'd moved, but he was a terror, thus his name. She'd originally named him Pumpkin because it was October when she'd adopted him from a box in front of New Seasons, but she should have listened to the man who was selling him and his litter. He'd told her that Loki was the most curious, most exploratory of all the kittens. She'd thought that sounded good at the time. She'd thought it would be fun. What it had meant was a lot of short nights in his kittenhood. It'd been a while since she'd woken up to a crash and plaintive meow, but in that first year, it had been a several times a night occurrence.

He didn't really want to escape, though. He wound around her feet and ankles, rubbing on her to say hello. Grace sank onto the old couch she kept on the porch, and he jumped up next to her so he could rub on her face and make biscuits on her lap. Grace was thankful she was wearing a knee-length skirt to protect herself from his claws.

"Hi, little man. It was another no for a roommate, but don't you worry. I have a plan to keep you in cat food."

He purred and worked the fabric of her skirt. She made a mental note to clip his claws soon. For now, she'd spend a moment on the porch, watching the world go by and snuggling her favorite guy in the world.

Chapter Two

Lenka obsessively checked her email for the fourth time in thirty minutes. Nothing. Well, nothing she wanted to see. She was supposed to fly to the US in less than two weeks for the school year, but so far, no host family had been found. She banged her head softly on the table. It had to be soft because it was a rickety table in her childhood room that was now a dumping ground for her parents' stuff. They'd kindly moved this table in for her to have something to put her laptop on, but she missed her big sturdy desk.

She'd been trying to stretch the time between fruitlessly checking emails, but she was waiting on a call from Mackenzie and didn't have anything else to do while she waited. Living at home with her parents in Louny didn't provide a lot of excitement. It was only for three weeks between summer term ending in Prague and leaving for the States. If she got a placement.

Lenka pushed back and paced. It was nerve-racking, waiting. She knew she wasn't the only one who hadn't gotten a placement yet, but she so envied those who had, particularly those who'd gotten placements in New York. That was her dream, living in New York where she could see her girlfriend every day, where she could start to make connections to get a job when she graduated at the end of this school year. If she passed her English test. Her English was good. Mackenzie always told her it was excellent, but it wasn't translator good, not yet.

That was another reason for needing to get a placement, preferably with a family. She wanted a family who sat around the table for dinner and talked. She needed that practice.

The distinctive ring of an incoming video chat had her rushing back to the table.

"Hey, baby." Mackenzie's face beamed at her from her screen. There was a lot of background noise and movement. Lenka could tell she was backstage, probably at one of the shared vanities her current off off-Broadway production provided.

Lenka wanted to reach into the screen and stroke her cheek. She settled for a smile and a return of the greeting. "Getting ready for tonight's show?"

Mackenzie pulled a face before looking away and applying foundation with a sponge. At least, that was what Lenka thought she was doing. Her knowledge of makeup was rudimentary at best. Mackenzie opened her mouth, stretching her face as she worked. Her voice was a little distorted when she said, "Yeah, and time is tight, so I'm going to have to cut this a little short."

Disappointment crashed through Lenka. They hadn't had a long talk in a couple of weeks, just stolen moments here and there. But part of that was probably Lenka's fault. She'd had end-of-term tests to take and was packing up and moving last week. This week, she just had too much downtime on her hands, and it was making her needy. She put a smile on her face. "I understand. Did you wait tables today, too?"

Mackenzie's acting jobs were sporadic and not well paying, so she served tables to make ends meet, as did most of New York's hopeful and semiprofessional actors, according to Mackenzie. "No. I met up with some castmates to discuss future possibilities." She lowered her voice and looked at her screen. "This one isn't long for the world."

While that was important, too, Lenka felt another stab of disappointment. She'd assumed Mackenzie had gotten held up at work, and that was why she was late for their talk. Again, she was just sensitive this week. It would all be better when they were together in New York.

"Have you heard about a host family yet?"

Lenka shook her head, then realized Mackenzie wouldn't see it because she was looking in the mirror. "No." She wished she could just live with her—not that Mackenzie had offered, exactly—but the rules of the exchange were clear. It had to be a host family, and in order to qualify, they had to have a bedroom for the exchange student. Mackenzie lived in a tiny studio apartment with a roommate. She couldn't register as a host family even if she wanted to. "Not yet. I—"

"Thank you, twenty," Mackenzie called along with many other voices. She turned to the screen. "Sorry, baby. I have to go. See you in a couple of weeks, I hope." She blew a quick kiss and hit the end call button before Lenka could reply.

A couple of weeks. Yes. Then they'd be together. It was the frustration of distance that was causing this feeling of unsettledness. She and Mackenzie were meant to be. It was destiny that they'd shared that train car from Paris to Brussels this spring. Destiny would insure that Lenka was in New York in two weeks, too.

She clicked to maximize her browser window and was finally rewarded with an email bearing the subject line, "Host family assignment."

Lenka stood, knocking her chair over in her excitement. She'd known it would happen—the program had promised a placement—but it finally being here was such a relief. She pumped her fists and jumped on her childhood bed. She waved her hands and danced like no one was looking. Finally, she sat back down to read the details.

Dear Lenka,

We are happy to inform you that we have found you a homestay match. Attached, you will find the details of your host family, including contact information. Also attached is your plane ticket. Congratulations on a match, and we hope you enjoy your exchange year in the United States.

Sincerely,
Mildred Hustler

Mildred was her program coordinator, and while they'd exchanged several more personal emails, this one was clearly a form letter. It was fine, though. The exciting part was the attachments.

Lenka hovered the mouse over the one that was clearly the airline ticket information, then over the one that was host family. Host family was more important. She could see the details of the ticket next. There were a couple of airlines that had direct flights, and a girl could dream, but again, that could wait. Whatever flight was fine. She clicked on the host family information attachment.

It took her a moment to orient to the information. The first couple of pages were a filled-out host family interview form. The next was a welcome letter. The last page simply contained a picture. It was of one woman who looked to be in her twenties standing in front of a house. There were a couple of things wrong with that picture. It wasn't the woman, who was very attractive, with dark hair and a sweet smile. It was that there was only one person, not a family, and she was expecting an apartment, not a house, certainly not with an overgrown yard. She scrolled back up to the interview. Yep. It was just one woman, Grace Talcott.

Lenka stuffed down her disappointment. It was fine. She'd figure out getting extra English practice if necessary. When she got to the part about where the home was located, she closed her laptop and lay her head down on it in defeat.

She was going to Portland, Oregon. A whole continent away from Mackenzie.

Chapter Three

Grace stood just outside of where passengers emerged from the gates as they arrived in Portland. She awkwardly held a sign in sparkling letters that said, "Welcome, Lenka!"

The last two and a half weeks had been a whirlwind. She'd gone through all the steps of the application in two days off from work. They'd been in a hurry and come to interview her and see the house at the same time. Once she'd cleared a background check, she was in.

Those two days had been wildly busy. The room had to be furnished. Grace's entire house was barely furnished. Between her lack of money and Loki's tendency to knock everything off any flat surface, it simply hadn't happened. She'd had to ask friends, get online and look at freebies and cheap furniture, and had finally managed a double bed, a set of drawers, a little table to use as a nightstand, and a lamp that clamped on to it that Loki couldn't knock over.

Then, she'd gone back to work to find that there was a horrible case of the flu running through all the nurses in the emergency department. She'd spent the last two weeks covering extra shifts, working at least twelve hours a day. She'd seen the email with her student assignment—*get ready to welcome Lenka from the Czech Republic*—but hadn't opened it. There hadn't been time. She also hadn't opened the email that explained about picking her up from the airport as of yesterday. That one had resulted in a text from

Mildred asking for verification of receipt. So she'd finally gone back and opened it and had made it here now.

The sign had been made by Maci, one of the people laid low by the flu. She had spent some of her bedridden time making it when she'd heard about how many shifts Grace was working.

So here she was, blearily standing under the display for arrivals and departures that had assured her that the plane Lenka was on had landed. She'd cleared passport control in Seattle, so she'd be coming out with regular domestic arrivals. Grace had never picked up anyone coming in internationally to PDX and wouldn't have known where to go. She supposed the email would have said if that was the case, but thinking about anything too deeply was hard. She was so very tired.

She'd just gotten off a shift that was supposed to end at seven—well, seven thirty by the time shift change was over—but had lasted until a little after eight and come straight here. At least she'd changed out of scrubs at the hospital, so she was wearing regular-person clothing. Besides, her last set of scrubs had encountered fluids that were commonplace to Grace but made the general public shudder. She'd checked her hair to make sure nothing untoward was in it. Things sometimes spurted. She was wearing it pulled back in a ponytail, as she always did for work. Her bangs had seemed…fine. She wouldn't scare this poor teenager from the Czech Republic. Probably. Unless the bags under her eyes were deep and purple enough to be a sign of the devil or something.

She sighed. She'd been open to a teen from anywhere, but when Maci had pointed out that homophobia was alive and well in various countries around the world, Grace had second-guessed that openness. When she'd seen Czech Republic, she'd felt some relief. She'd thought it would be okay. That was until one of the floating nurses filling in for a sick ED nurse had told her that some of the formally Soviet nations still weren't very LGBTQ+ friendly. She'd immigrated from Poland with her parents as a teenager, and her grandparents were appalled she'd *turned out gay*. So now, Grace was worried again. Well, maybe she'd be a one-woman mind-opening experience for Lenka.

There was a stream of passengers coming out now, and Grace hoped one of them would be Lenka. She was so tired, and her feet hurt so much. She just wanted to collapse into bed and sleep for fourteen hours. Tomorrow would be her first day off in thirteen days, and she was so ready for it. Lenka would likely be exhausted, too, and they could just sleep and veg together for the day. It would be a good bonding experience.

Wait. She'd never opened the email that had introduced Lenka, so she had no idea what she looked like. Shit. She dropped one end of the sign and fished in her pocket for her phone. A petite woman who definitely wasn't a teenager and with pink hair in a bedraggled ponytail stopped in front of her. She had a sprinkling of freckles across her nose and cheeks and was about the most breathtakingly adorable woman Grace had ever laid eyes on.

"Grace?"

"Um, do we know each other?" She was sure she would have remembered.

The pink-haired woman gestured at the sign. "I'm Lenka."

Grace nearly fell over from shock. There was no way. There was no way she was in high school.

Lenka touched her hair. "Yeah, there was a color change. It was purple when the picture was taken, but…are you okay?"

Grace forced a smile. Okay, she'd misunderstood. She thought she was hosting a teenager, but she was hosting a…college student? Despite the pink hair, small stature, and freckles, Lenka seemed older than that. She seemed confident and mature. Grace, meanwhile, felt like a stumbling child. "Well, welcome. Sorry, I've been working a lot and was distracted. I…" She held up the sign. "Welcome. Like the sign says. Okay, then, let's go get your bags." She started for the escalators that led to baggage claim. "I'm sure you must be tired."

"I am, yes." Lenka's accent was not strong. Grace had expected her to be harder to understand. Again, she had to readjust her expectations. "But excited to be here." She didn't sound super excited, but it was probably jet lag.

They stepped onto the escalator. "I lucked out with a good parking spot, so we'll just collect your bags and get home. Do you have a lot? What am I asking? Of course you do. You're here for ten months." She checked out the monitors at the foot of the escalator. "Okay, looks like baggage carrousel three. This way." For some reason, she continued to babble. "My car isn't huge, but it's a hatchback, and the seats fold down, so we can fit plenty in there. It'll be no problem. My car is a reliable little thing. It has to be to get me to work."

She continued to talk while they waited, going on inanely to cover her wrong-footedness at the start. She caught Lenka side-eyeing her a couple of times but couldn't seem to stop the verbal geyser. She was relieved when Lenka's bags finally ambled around the conveyer. She pulled one of the two, large, heavy bags back to the escalator. There was probably more in these bags than Grace owned, aside from the sparse furniture.

And she just kept talking. "We'll go back up the escalator. I parked on four, which is the level with the sky bridge. It's where departures are, but the sky bridge is cool, and we don't have to deal with elevators. So up we go." Her cheeks burned. Did she think she was talking to a toddler? To cover, she kept going: "It's only about a fifteen minute drive home, then we can both crash. Did I mention I'm super tired, too? I've been working a lot."

When they finally made it home, Grace babbling on the entire way, she showed Lenka to her room. She tried to grab the laminated page of rules off the set of drawers without Lenka seeing, but Lenka reached out a hand. "Is this for me?"

"Oh, um…" Grace didn't know how to get out of handing it over. It was clearly for Lenka, but it had been created with the idea of a teenager in mind. The rules were ridiculous for this adult, put-together woman. "Yes, kind of, but not really. It's no big deal."

Lenka took the page and looked at it curiously.

Grace hurriedly said, "Make yourself at home. Bathroom's across the hall. Kitchen is downstairs. I'll see you tomorrow." She rushed out and went into her own room, closing the door gratefully behind her.

She barely made it through her shower before falling asleep practically as her head hit the pillow.

She woke up to her phone ringing at six a.m. She was going to kill whoever it was. She was supposed to get to sleep in this morning. But the events of the night before rushed back in, and she answered, hoping it was a call into work so she could avoid the stranger she'd embarrassed herself in front of the night before and was now living in her home.

"'ello?" Her voice was croaky from yet another short night of sleep.

"Hey, Grace. I'm so sorry to do this to you, but it seems the flu isn't done with us yet. Are you still healthy, and can you come in today?"

"Sure. No problem." Anything to get out of the house.

Chapter Four

When Lenka woke up, she didn't have one of those "where am I" moments. She'd never had one, and she'd traveled a fair amount. Well, in Europe, at least. This was her first time in America. Still, she was aware of where she was from the moment she opened her eyes. America. But not New York. Oregon. Portland, Oregon. Northeast Portland, Oregon. She'd spent a lot of time looking at Google Maps with the pin in Grace's house, wondering how it would be. And now she knew.

It would be weird.

She imagined some of that would pass as she became accustomed to this bed, this house, this city, this person. Grace had been very, very chatty. It'd been kind of cute. Lenka somehow hadn't expected that from the picture. In person, Grace was a little disheveled but still quite good-looking. Lenka had imagined conversation but not the endless flow of words Grace had produced. As cute as it had been, it had been a lot for how tired Lenka was. She hadn't kept up with everything, much less gotten a word in edgewise. Grace was probably nervous having a stranger move in with her, and Lenka was hoping today would be a little smoother.

She'd slept like a rock, exhausted from jet lag. It was dinner time back in Prague, but the sun had the brightness of late morning. That was strange on its own. Wasn't it supposed to rain all the time here? All in all, everything felt a little surreal.

But she was only three hours off of Mackenzie's time zone now, which was pretty cool. She pulled her phone off the little nightstand and video called her.

"Hey, baby. We're in the same country. How are you? Did you just wake up? I love a sleep-tousled Lenka." She bit her lip in a way that had Lenka wishing she was here in this bed, too. Not that that could happen. It was against the exchange policy to have overnight guests. If—when—she did come to visit, they'd be staying in a hotel.

"Hey, zlatíčko. I'm okay. I slept a lot. I feel a little…disoriented." Lenka wasn't sure that was the right word. She definitely knew where she was. But also things didn't feel quite right.

Mackenzie gave a sympathetic face. "To be expected. You'll adjust, right? And I'll be there to visit you before you know it."

Lenka smiled, even though they hadn't set a time yet. "I can't wait."

Mackenzie looked away, held up a finger to indicate waiting for a minute, and turned back. "I've gotta go. We were just about to head out to meet the gang for a late lunch before call time. Talk soon, baby." And she was gone.

Okay, then. It was time to tackle being here, adjusting to this house, and getting to know her host mom. Lenka laughed aloud at that. She wouldn't be calling Grace that. She was two years older than her, who was just old enough to be eligible to host, and Lenka had gone back to school to pursue becoming a translator after deciding that working in the hospitality sector was not for her.

However, they could be friends. Maybe. If Grace wasn't too rule bound. It was an extensive list she'd given Lenka the night before. Not that they were unreasonable. Who would turn on the heat and open the window? Also, Lenka was fine with not hoarding used dishes in her room. It was a long and oddly detailed list, though.

It didn't matter. Lenka was going to give her a chance, more than that. Grace had opened her home and given Lenka a spot. Sure, it wasn't New York, but it was in the US. Lenka would work hard on her English and earn a spot translating for the United Nations. Then, she'd live in New York with Mackenzie. It was just a delay of a year, but it would still happen. And it started with getting up and making conversation.

Lenka slipped into the hall, not wanting to bump into Grace before using the bathroom and washing up. But when she was done, she realized she was home alone. She'd thought that one of the many things Grace had said the night before was that they could both sleep in today because Grace was off. Maybe she'd misunderstood, or maybe Grace was out running an errand.

She looked around the kitchen to figure out the coffee situation and found a note next to the coffee maker. *Got called into work. Make yourself at home.*

Lenka's heart sank. So much for a built-in conversational partner. She was going to have to go out and try to meet people. School would make that easier, but it didn't start for two weeks. Maybe Grace would be around some, but Lenka was going to have a lot of time to fill.

She was on her way back to her room to get properly dressed when something dashed by her in the hall. She nearly jumped out of her skin before she remembered that Grace had a cat. Loki. That was it. She followed him down the hall, thinking to at least make friends with him, only to find he'd gone into Grace's room. She wasn't about to invade her bedroom, even to make friends with the little brown-and-black cat she saw staring at her from Grace's bed.

It seemed no one in this house wanted to hang out with her. She turned back to her room, trying not to feel sorry for herself. She did know someone who would be excited to talk to her. It wasn't too late in France, and anyway, Grand-mere was something of a night owl. She'd also mastered video calls when Lenka was a teenager so they could keep in touch between visits. Lenka went back to her room and hit the call button.

"Lenka, darling, how are you?" She spoke in French, of course. It was because of her that Lenka's French was as good as it was.

"Good, Grand-mere," Lenka answered in the same language. "I got some sleep and am ready to take on the world." It was only a slight exaggeration.

"That's my girl. How do you like Grace?"

Lenka told her what she knew of her host while she finished getting ready for the day. She'd decided to treat herself to coffee out. It was her first day in country, and it would get her out talking to people. At least she'd get to practice with the barista.

They chatted about the flight and about Grand-mere's neighbors. She was close with a couple of them and friendly with most. But one of her particular friends had passed away recently, and her grandson had moved into her house with his wife and two small children.

"It's giving the neighborhood a much needed infusion of new life," Grand-mere said with a nod, as if convincing herself. Lenka knew she missed her friend but also refused to cut herself off from new experiences. It was one of the things she admired about her. "The children are adorable. I've told them to come over for fresh baked goodies anytime."

"Of course you did, Grand-mere." Lenka beamed at her.

After a few minutes more, Grand-mere gently pushed Lenka to follow through with her plan to go out and explore, claiming she was going to bed anyway. Lenka knew she'd be up for quite a while longer but didn't push back. She did need to get out there. They said their good-byes, and Lenka walked to Alberta, a street a few blocks south that Google had told her was rife with restaurants and shops.

It was nearly noon by the time she got there, and the street was hopping with foot traffic. There were some restaurants with excellent smells and plenty of customers using the outdoor seating on this lovely late summer day. Her stomach reminded her that it was dinnertime as far as it was concerned, and she'd skipped both breakfast and lunch. Food did sound good, but what drew her in first was a coffee shop with a large Pride flag draped in one window. It was far from the first one she'd seen on the street, which was really living up to its online reputation as the gay district of Portland—if one didn't consider all of Portland to be the gay district—but it was the first one with the aroma of coffee drifting into the street. It also had outdoor seating. Lenka was sold.

The barista had a lot of creative piercings and took her order with a wink. When she got to the name, though, she looked at Lenka in bewilderment. Lenka spelled it for her, wondering if she should have given a Starbucks name, something she'd never had to do at home.

"It's a lovely name," the barista said. "Where are you from?"

"Thanks. I'm from Czechia, the Czech Republic." Lenka didn't get why English speakers couldn't just say Czechia. The Czech Republic was such a mouthful.

"Oh. Where's that?"

Lenka wondered at the American school system, but she gamely explained it was in Europe next to Germany.

"Really? That's so cool. Are you here on vacation?"

Lenka was a little surprised by her chattiness, but considering she'd come out of the house for just this sort of interaction, she wasn't complaining. But she felt a little bad about the couple of people in line behind her. Still, she answered a couple more questions before her name, or more accurately, a facsimile of her name, was called at the other end. Lenka might have been imagining it, but she thought that barista said it a little pointedly, as if reminding Willa—according to the name tag on her apron—that she'd spent that whole time chatting instead of working.

"I guess I'll be seeing a lot of you. Welcome to Portland," Willa called as Lenka waved good-bye and went to collect her drink.

Lenka wasn't sure about that. The exchange program had been expensive, and she didn't have a lot of extras for this sort of thing, as much as she'd like to come here every day. The coffee was as excellent as it smelled, which only made her more interested. She'd have to really school herself to stick to her budget. She settled with her coffee at a table outside and watched the people go by, who were also excellent.

She was in a much better mood after some more strolling on Alberta and treating herself to a burrito from a cart. She really, really couldn't do this all the time, she reminded herself, even as she took her first delicious bite. But that was a problem for her future self. Her today self deserved a little pampering.

She found a little bookshop with a lot of used books and a significant LGBTQ+ section. She bought one. It was used, after all, and she could sell it back when she was done. Plus, she needed to work on her English. It was practically a school expense.

As she walked up the block to further explore, she was hit with a wave of tiredness. For all she'd slept well and long, her body was sure it was the middle of the night now. She decided to head back to Grace's house. Maybe she would be home from work, and they'd have dinner together.

But the house was empty when Lenka got there. She held off on dinner, hoping Grace would show up, and eventually fell asleep reading her book.

CHAPTER FIVE

How're things going with Lenka?" Maci asked.

Maci and Grace were sitting at the nurse's station doing paperwork during a rare lull in patients. Grace didn't really even have much paperwork to do. She was stretching what little there was. It didn't do to look non-busy in the ED. It was inviting a catastrophe. She made a note while she considered how to answer.

"I mean," Maci continued, "you're always here. So it can't possibly be going well. Are you leaving that poor girl to fend for herself in a new city?"

"She's not a girl."

"What?" Maci squinted at her. "You're not making some sort of horrible transphobic statement, are you?" She swiveled in her chair and grabbed Grace's shoulders, giving her a little shake. "Who are you, and what have you done with my best friend?"

Grace held her hands up in self-defense. "No, of course not. I mean, she's not a teenager. She's older than me."

Maci dropped Grace's shoulders and waved to a passing doctor who was looking at them with a mix of amusement and alarm. "But she's in high school?"

Grace covered her face with her hands. "No. She's in college. And she's a returning college student. All of which I'd have known if the flu hadn't decimated us in the weeks before her arrival. I didn't even realize it was a possibility, having a college student. And then, I made a fool of myself when I picked her up."

"I see. You've been hiding out here. Taking every extra shift. I know we're understaffed, but I even heard you ask Linda if she wanted the first day of school for her kids off. Not just taking them, looking for them."

Grace spread two fingers and peeked at her. "Yes?"

"Okay, so you're hiding out from this older woman who is living in your house because…"

Grace removed her hands from her face only to throw them in the air. "I told you, I made a fool of myself on that first night. Besides. I still need the money. And she's twenty-seven. She's plenty old enough to fend for herself. It's now just a roommate situation. That's just what it is. Besides, I'm not hiding out. I've seen her. A few times."

Grace could count the number of times. The second morning Lenka had been in the house, she'd been up before Grace. Jet lag, probably. Grace had mumbled a good morning as she'd gotten her coffee before scooting out the door. There had been a couple of evenings more lately, a little over a week in. Lenka was probably adjusting to the time and staying up later now. They'd exchanged greetings, and Grace had rallied herself to say that Lenka could add to the shopping list on the fridge if she needed anything. Lenka had seemed like she wanted to talk more, but Grace had yawned a not-fake yawn and said she needed to go to bed.

Maci narrowed her eyes again. "That sounds like a lot of justification. Would you be hiding out from a regular roommate? There's something else, isn't there?"

Grace went back to her paperwork, but she could feel her cheeks heat. Maci must have been able to see it, too, because she slapped Grace on her shoulder. "She's cute, isn't she?"

Grace's cheeks got hotter. "Maybe. But it doesn't matter."

"You are hiding out because you made a fool of yourself in front of an attractive woman."

"And I need the money," Grace protested.

"Sure, sure. Okay, well, that poor woman is having to find her own way with no friends, no nothing. And you signed up to be a host mom." Maci started giggling. "Host mom. To a person who is a couple of years older." She burst into actual laughter. "You have to admit, that's funny."

"Ha, ha, hilarious. If it had happened to someone else." But Maci's words about her responsibility to Lenka creeped into her mind and made her uncomfortable. She should make an effort to get home earlier more often.

Still, when patients from a multiple car crash came in just before the end of Grace's shift, she rushed in to help.

❖

A couple of days later, the charge nurse showed up at the desk and announced that someone needed to go early. Were there any volunteers? She looked right at Grace as she said it. One of the other nurses started to raise her hand, but the charge nurse ignored her. "Grace. Excellent. Your hours have been getting out of hand. Go home and rest up."

It was time to face the music. It was only five, so Grace put off the inevitable by getting the grocery shopping done on the way home. Lenka had only added things Grace stocked anyway, clearly putting them on the list as they ran out or got near to. Grace would hardly know. With the hours she'd been keeping, she only used coffee, bread, and sandwich stuff. A real meal would have been lovely. Maybe she'd cook when she got home. She gathered herself. She could cook for herself and Lenka. She was supposed to be feeding the woman, after all.

But when she got home, Lenka was out. It was a relief. But also a worry. At some point, she'd have to face the music and get past her initial embarrassment. And signs were developing that she wasn't going to be able to hide at work forever with the charge nurse having sent her home in addition to the new nurse who had started earlier this week. Rumor had it that another was going to start next week. The staffing issues were leveling out, and her charge nurse had clearly noticed how much Grace was working. She'd been allowed when it was truly necessary, but one person working a bunch of shifts meant paying overtime, which was expensive for the hospital. Grace wasn't surprised that the last month was being noticed.

She unloaded groceries, then decided on a frozen meal because it was easy, and she was tired. She sat on the couch to eat and watch something. It was a series she'd been working her way through, but it had been so long since she'd watched that she barely remembered what was happening or why she liked this show. Loki snuggled into her lap, clearly starved for attention. She was messing up all over the place. Poor Loki.

Shortly after she finished eating, she fell asleep.

When she woke up in the middle of the night with a full bladder, it was to a dark house and the realization that the throw blanket from the back of the couch had been placed over her. Or maybe she'd drawn it over herself in her half-awake state? She was pretty sure she hadn't. This was ridiculous. Lenka was taking care of her when it was supposed to be the other way around. Grace had to get her shit together.

She threw the blanket aside, accidentally unseating Loki, who glared balefully at her before running down the hall. Grace met him in her bed after a visit to the bathroom.

She settled in with him in the curve of her knees, made sure to set the alarm for her morning shift, and fell back asleep while resolving to work normal person hours—as much as was possible as a hospital nurse—and maybe show Lenka around Portland before she started school.

Chapter Six

"Hi, zlatíčko." Lenka smiled at her screen. She and Mackenzie had talked regularly, but Mackenzie was always busy running to one job or the other. Today, though, the theater was dark. It was Monday. Mackenzie's roommate was out of town for a long weekend. And she had worked the lunch shift. So they were planning a nice, long conversation. Lenka, who'd been at loose ends since she got to Portland, was thrilled.

"Hey, baby." Mackenzie smiled back at her. "How's Portland?"

"I mostly like the city, what I've seen of it. I'm living near Alberta, which is incredibly gay friendly. Pride flags and same-sex couples holding hands everywhere. I found a coffee shop I love. I've figured out my route to school and back. Oh! This is exciting. I went to the library, thinking I'd just read there, and they said I could get a library card, so that's excellent. Even the library is gay friendly. The librarian I talked to was wearing a Pride pin, and they have quite the selection of lesbian romances."

Loki strolled into her room, clearly roused by her voice. He jumped on her bed, arched his back in a stretch and stared at her. She reached out to scratch his head, but he ducked away. Clearly, he was in a playing, not petting, mood.

Mackenzie's smile turned indulgent. "You do love your books. So what does the mostly part mean?"

Lenka picked up the string she kept on the nightstand under her current book and swished it through the air over his head. "Well, I knew that there were homeless people in the US, but I never really understood how that looked. There are a lot of people who don't have homes here, and I don't really know what to do about it."

Mackenzie waved that off. "It's just a fact of life. People choose to live on the streets rather than follow the rules of society. You just have to ignore them."

That didn't sound right, but it was true that Lenka didn't know what to do to help. She felt powerless. There had been an orientation put on by Overseas Stays on the first Saturday she'd been in Portland. They'd addressed the homeless situation, telling the students to simply ignore the people on the streets, be they begging, camping, ranting, or some combination. That also didn't feel right. She supposed the problem was beyond her to solve.

Maybe there was some sort of volunteering she could do while she was here, if not directly with homeless, at least with people in need. If nothing else, it would give her more English practice, which would be good. Particularly since she wasn't getting practice at home.

That had been another thing that had come up at the orientation, questions about how everyone was settling in with their host families. People had talked about their families taking them to see Multnomah Falls or to the big Powell's Bookstore downtown. Other people had talked about playing with their host siblings or new meals they'd tried. Lenka had just stayed quiet. She had nothing to contribute. She was sore about it. But also, she was a full-grown woman, and if anyone was going to end up with someone who ignored them, it was good it was her, really. She just needed to find other ways to practice English.

Loki swiped at her bare knee to remind her that she was supposed to be entertaining him. She dutifully pulled the string across the bed. He looked at it, then sat to clean himself, apparently uninterested.

"Anything else?"

Lenka pulled her attention back to her girlfriend and the conversation at hand. She couldn't figure out what the question was in reference to, though. "About homeless people? Because, yeah, a little. I don't get how so many more people in America don't want to follow society's rules than other places. We have a few homeless people in Czechia, but it's hardly any."

"Hmm, I don't really know. Anyway. What about a visit? Should we plan one?"

"Of course. I can't wait to see you. When can you come?"

Loki stared at her, unimpressed with her enthusiasm and hopped off the bed.

Mackenzie thrust out her lower lip in a pout. Lenka wanted to suck on it. It was very tempting. It was so frustrating not seeing her in person. "I was hoping you could come here. I'm ever so busy."

"I can't. It's against the program rules. I mean, I can, but not until on the way home. Or if I signed up for a group trip that goes to New York, but that's super expensive, and I'd have to stay with the group. It makes me feel like a teenager having all these rules." She winced at both her own whining and the crash she heard in the hall. Loki was clearly knocking things around. He was a little wild, that cat.

"Yeah. It feels like I'm dating one, too."

Lenka tried not to take that personally. After all, she was the one who'd invited the comparison in the first place.

Mackenzie cocked her head. "The taskmaster is kind of hot, right?" She smiled with a hint of mischief. "Should I be worried?"

Lenka agreed with the hot part. Every time she saw Grace, she couldn't help but notice it. She had a girlfriend, but she wasn't dead. And taskmaster seemed sort of apt. There was that list of rules she still had tucked away. One of which had been a rule about no sleeping on the couch, and yet, she'd come home to find her sleeping there the other night. It had been a sweet picture, her with a hand tucked under her cheek, very softly snoring, and Loki curled against her. She'd covered her before retreating to her room.

She felt a little affronted at the idea of Grace being rule bound. If anything, she was hands off more than strict. The idea that the younger Grace could be strict was kind of funny, really. "She's never even here, so there's nothing to worry about. We should worry about when you can visit instead."

"I think the first time I can come is in November. The show run ends in October."

They talked details for a while, deciding that when Lenka was on break from school for Christmas was the best time for a visit. Then, they shared little details of their days. Lenka said she'd met a couple of people at the orientation and had gotten together with them a few times now. It was good to have people to explore the city with. And since they all came from different countries, English was their common language, so it was also good practice. Lenka and Sue had been on all of those excursions and had hit it off. The group had been limited to places they could reach via bus or bike rental because as exchange students, they weren't permitted to drive.

Mackenzie shared all the little dramas of stage and restaurant. As usual, her humor was sometimes cutting, but Lenka almost always thought it was funny. She knew Mackenzie had a good heart, so it was easy to excuse her when things sometimes crossed the line.

As they were wrapping up so Mackenzie could get ready to meet some friends for dinner, she asked, "When do classes start again?"

"I'm already doing the translation course through my sending school, but local school starts Wednesday. Day after tomorrow. I can't wait."

Mackenzie smiled at her. "You're such a nerd. I couldn't wait to be done with school."

"I know school isn't for everyone, but I do love learning. But a lot of my excitement is that I'm looking forward to meeting people. I need friends to practice my English with so I can pass the test and move to New York."

"That is a priority." Mackenzie pumped her eyebrows. "I need to see you in person. I have designs on your body."

Lenka felt a throb of desire at the words. She touched a finger to the neckline of the top she was wearing. She moved it slowly in what she hoped was a seductive manner. She looked up at the door to her room, wondering if she should lock it.

Mackenzie bit her lip. "I'd love to play, but I really have to get going."

Lenka dropped her hand. "Fine. Go have fun with your friends."

Mackenzie huffed a laugh. "I will. But think of me while you do...whatever you're going to do next."

But after they hung up, Lenka's thoughts turned away from Mackenzie's charms and toward classes starting on Wednesday. She opened her browser and logged into Portland State University's student website. While all the exchange students with her program were going to school there, they were each pursuing their own lines of study. So she wasn't going to have classes with any of the people she'd met.

One of hers was a French seminar. Her French was very good thanks to her grand-mere, who she'd spent summers with growing up. Because of that and because she was in an English-speaking country, English was what she was concentrating on. Since all classes were in English, that meant she could take anything and get the credits she needed for her degree at her sending school. She'd come on exchange still needing a few French credits but mostly needing English ones.

Loki jumped back up onto her bed and dropped a toy on her lap. It was one of the things off the almond milk that showed it had been sealed until that moment. Most people threw these away, but Lenka understood why Grace didn't. Loki loved them. He had many of them scattered about the house. She threw it for him, and he raced after it.

Lenka looked back at her screen. In addition to the French seminar, she was taking a three-hundred level English class called Topics in Lesbian and Womxn Identities in Literature, a three-hundred level linguistics class called Structure of the English Language, and Introduction to Intercultural Communication. She'd taken Introduction to Intercultural Communication at her sending school as well, but she thought it would be interesting to approach the subject from an American perspective.

She had three of the four classes on Wednesday. It was a long day at school. Tuesdays and Thursdays were short days, and she had no Friday classes. She'd rather have spread things out, but that was what had worked out. It was fine. She'd find a volunteer opportunity that she could do on Fridays or over the weekends. That would help fill in the gaps of time.

Meanwhile, tomorrow, she and her exchange friends were going to the zoo. One of them had gone with his host family and said it was great. Lenka was looking forward to it. She sent Sue a text asking which animal she wanted to see first.

Loki showed back up with the almond milk thingy in his mouth. Lenka stroked his back before she threw it again. He was very cute and made her feel like she wasn't alone when she was home, even if he disappeared at night, presumably to sleep with Grace.

Sue texted back a GIF of an elephant.

She was figuring this out. She'd make it work. Even with a host family that had turned out to be an absent roommate.

Chapter Seven

Grace yawned and stretched. It was her first time sleeping in in way too long. It felt luxurious, but she also felt a little groggy from sleeping so long. She picked up her phone to check the time. Her eyes widened in surprise, and she sat up quickly, causing Loki to scramble for a hold on her blanket before giving up and face-butting her. It was ten. She'd planned on getting up around eight, making breakfast for Lenka, and offering to take her to a few favorite places around the city. She'd checked through the slew of emails from the exchange organization yesterday to figure out when classes started. Wednesday. So today was the last day she could act as the host she was supposed to be.

Once she'd run through her bathroom routine and gone to the kitchen to figure out food and coffee, she realized Lenka wasn't home. Okay, so she was clearly working out her own adjustment to living in Portland and didn't need Grace.

She got Loki's food out. She was surprised he hadn't woken her up to eat. She usually filled his bowl in the mornings. It was already full, though. Either he wasn't eating, which was highly unlikely, or Lenka had filled it.

Okay, okay. Grace had said she was going to treat Lenka like a roommate. She could still do that. They were clearly finding their own rhythms. Lenka was very considerate. Grace would be, too.

To start with, she left a note thanking Lenka for feeding Loki and leaving her cell phone number. They currently had no way to get in contact outside of notes or randomly running into each other.

She decided to enjoy her day off by treating herself to coffee and a scone at her favorite coffee shop. Her favorite barista was there, too. Grace thought she was attractive with all those piercings and enjoyed a short flirt while she ordered. She figured that Willa flirted with everyone, though, and didn't take it seriously. She suspected that Willa was genuinely open and friendly but also that the flirting didn't exactly hurt tips. She gave a generous one herself as she paid.

She settled at one of the outdoor tables and people-watched while she enjoyed her treat. September meant cool mornings, but the daytime temperatures could still get quite hot. It was lovely weather, with morning clouds burning off and temps in mid-seventies. She lingered for quite a while, eventually pulling out her phone to catch up with the wider world.

While Grace got a text from an unknown number that turned out to be Lenka thanking her for leaving her number the next day, it was Sunday before Grace actually saw her. She knew Lenka had been around because things moved in the house. They must have shared an affection for the throw over the back of the couch because while Grace tended to toss it back there haphazardly, she often found it folded neatly. She thought that maybe Lenka was just a neat freak, but she'd also caught a scent of vanilla on the blanket. Grace was partial to a lemon-scented shampoo, so she knew it must be from a product Lenka used. Maybe she should consider vanilla. It was nice.

Lenka did a lot of little thoughtful things like folding the throw, feeding Loki, emptying the dishwasher, and vacuuming. It was nice, but it also made Grace feel a little guilty. She'd thought she was going to be the adult in the hosting situation, but that was clearly Lenka.

She must have been keeping herself busy. Even though Grace had gotten home on time all week, which usually meant about eight, thinking maybe she'd catch Lenka, she was never there. To be fair, she usually ate a quick bite and went to bed. Twelve-hour days were long days, and she came home tired even when she didn't stay late. So Lenka might well have been home by nine, and Grace wouldn't know.

To be honest, she was still picking up extra shifts. Seeing as how Lenka wasn't around, Grace figured she should keep this moneymaking streak going.

Sunday, she was off again and again slept in, but this time when she woke up, she heard sounds from the kitchen. The smell of something sweet joined the sounds when she opened her door. She padded down the hall to investigate.

Grace stopped in the kitchen doorway, arrested by the image of Lenka swaying a little and bobbing her head. Presumably, she was listening to music through her earbuds. She shimmied a little, and Grace giggled at how cute it was. She bent to open the oven door, and Grace had to look away so as not to stare inappropriately. The aroma that filled the kitchen had her craning to see what was in there. "Oh my God, that smells amazing."

Lenka jumped about a foot in the air and spun around. She pulled out her earbuds and tucked them in a pocket. "Oh, I'm sorry. I didn't know you were home. I didn't mean to wake you."

Grace put her hands up to show she was unarmed. "No, I'm sorry. I know I've been gone a lot. You had no way of knowing."

Lenka shuffled a little, then turned and finished pulling a tray of pastries out of the oven. They looked amazing. There were little pools of what looked like jam in the middle of each. Grace moved closer to check out the ones already cooling.

"You can have one," Lenka said from closer than Grace expected. "All you want, in fact."

Grace found herself leaning in a little like she would with a friend before she caught herself. She moved away and poured a cup of coffee. Lenka must have made that, too. She went to the fridge to get the almond milk. "Thanks, but I don't want to eat them all up if you're making them for a reason." Her voice lifted at the end, making it a question.

"No, no. Just a Sunday morning project. I thought I'd leave them as a thank-you."

"Oh, you don't have to do that." She really didn't. Grace had mixed feelings about the gesture. She liked that someone was taking care of her, but she also felt guilty because that was supposed to be her job.

"I wanted to. You're letting me stay in your home."

Loki appeared, weaving between Grace's legs, rubbing against her. She set down her coffee and scooped him up. "There you are, little monster."

"He came out and wanted food earlier. I hope that's okay. That I fed him."

Grace had let him out of her room early this morning after he'd woken her up rubbing his face on her chin, then had upped the ante when she didn't get up by swatting her face. "Of course. Thank you. I've noticed you've been feeding him, and I'm sure he appreciates it."

"I wasn't sure if you'd forgotten to feed him before you went to work or he just ate a lot this morning. Let me know if you don't want me to."

"No, really. You can feed him anytime." Loki twisted, indicating he wanted down, and Grace let him go. He jumped up on the counter and sniffed at the pastries. "No, sir," Grace said to him. "Sorry. He has no manners."

"It's okay." She stroked his back. "He's sweet."

"A sweet little devil child, yes."

There seemed to be nothing more to say. This whole thing had turned out so differently than she'd expected. Not that she'd had a lot of time to paint herself a picture of hosting during the whirlwind that was the few weeks before Lenka had showed up, but she had imagined herself cooking if anyone was and maybe feeling needed. Lenka didn't need her.

Grace took a pastry with a thanks and took it and her coffee to the porch to people watch. Loki followed and settled on her lap. She considered how the interaction had gone. It was okay. They could do this roommate thing. Grace would live her life, and Lenka would live her own. They'd occasionally interact when their paths crossed.

And when this year was over, Grace would find a roommate that she wasn't attracted to and didn't feel any sort of obligation to be more than a roommate to. No more hosting. Unless it was dinner parties for her friends. At least she knew where she stood with them, and they generally left before things got awkward.

CHAPTER EIGHT

"This one." Lenka pointed. "This is definitely the one."

Sue cocked her head. "Are you sure this time?"

"I am." Lenka had made her choice. She bent and picked up the pumpkin. She'd never carved one before, but when Sue and her host family had offered to take her along to the pumpkin patch, she'd happily agreed. She was always looking to do an activity, especially one that let her practice her English. And this pumpkin was a perfect orange, not too big and not too small. She hefted it a few times, then held it on her hip with one hand. "This is it."

"Perfect."

Sue's ten-year-old host sister came to grab Sue's hand and take her to see the pumpkin she wanted. Lenka trailed along after. She still wished she had a host family like this. She wanted a kid talking to her a mile a minute about anything and everything.

Not that living with Grace was bad. If she was looking for just a roommate, Grace would have been about perfect. She kept to herself but was polite and considerate. These days, Lenka was intrigued by her and wanted to get to know her more, but she was not around much. They'd worked out chore distribution mostly by feel. Loki was entertaining. It was fine. But she was still out hunting opportunities to speak English. Like right now.

"What made you decide to host an exchange student?" Lenka asked Sue's host mom, who'd fallen in step beside her, trailing Sue and her host sister.

"Emma is in a Mandarin immersion school, so we've hosted a Mandarin speaker every year for five years now. It has helped her tremendously. This is our second year hosting a college student rather than a high schooler, which was also fun but a little more work. Sue is very independent. What made you decide to come here on exchange?"

They talked about Lenka's plans as a translator as Emma and Sue finished picking their pumpkins. Then, the whole group rode the tractor train back to pay. They dumped the pumpkins in the back of their station wagon, and Lenka thought the trip was over.

"Everyone up for apple cider doughnuts?" Sue's host dad asked.

"I am! I am!" Emma jumped up and down.

Lenka couldn't blame her. That sounded delicious. And they were. So was the warm apple cider, even though it was in the high sixties and sunny. And it turned out there was a corn maze to navigate. And a petting zoo that consisted entirely of goats. Lenka had no idea it would be this involved, but she was loving every minute.

At least, right up until they got in the car to go. Just getting out of the parking lot took about fifteen minutes. When they finally managed it, they were deposited in a long line of cars moving very slowly.

"Unfortunately, it's always like this getting off of Sauvie Island," Sue's host mom told them. "It's just part of the adventure."

"Let's play a game," Emma said. She was sitting in between Sue and Lenka in the back seat.

"What kind of game?" Sue asked.

They settled on Twenty Questions but did different categories in rounds. It took nearly an hour to get off the island, but it wasn't a problem for Lenka, who was happy to have a taste of family life. Once they'd escaped Sauvie Island, they stopped for dinner. Sue and Emma convinced her to come home with them to watch *Hocus Pocus* while they carved their pumpkins.

It was a great day. And she was only a little bit jealous that it wasn't her host family. Too bad she didn't speak Mandarin.

She took the bus home, arriving at nearly ten. It wasn't that late, but she'd noticed that on the evenings that Grace worked, she came home and practically went straight to bed. So Lenka snuck in without turning on a light.

She went to the kitchen for a glass of water before making her way down the hall to her room. She was pleased with her day and looking forward to writing a long message to Grand-mere telling her all about it. She'd get a kick out of the American tradition of carving pumpkins.

Then, a furry little body twined around her ankles, there was a horrible cat noise, and she was falling over.

Her first thought was: Shit, that's going to wake Grace up. Her second thought was: Ouch, oh fuck, ouch.

She rolled over to her back, causing further stabbing pains in her arm. She looked at it in the dim ambient light, half expecting to have a second elbow, but it looked normal. It just hurt like fuck.

Loki poked his head out from Grace's bedroom as if wondering if the fuss was over. He seemed to be fine, despite the howl he'd let out at their contact. There was no point yelling at him. He'd just been acting like a cat. And with Grace's bedroom door open, that meant she was not home. That wasn't great. Lenka could use a nurse's opinion about if her arm was broken. It felt like it. It hurt like hell. But it looked normal, so maybe it would pass.

She used her good arm to push up and scooted to rest her back against the hall with her hurt arm cradled to her chest. She'd wait a bit and see if the pain ebbed.

Loki sauntered down the hall, apparently convinced all was okay. He stopped in front of her as if to ask why she was sitting here. Then, he moved closer and rubbed on her. When he brushed her elbow, she gasped in pain. Loki gave her an affronted look and ran off.

Well. That wasn't good. She was going to have to get herself to the hospital for X-rays. She hadn't ever looked carefully at her insurance information. She was young and healthy. She hadn't expected to need medical care the entire time she was here.

Gritting her teeth against the anticipation of pain, she pushed up to standing. She had to pause and wait for a few moments catching her breath, good hand braced on the wall. It had to be broken. What else would be causing this much pain in the middle of her forearm? Shit, shit, shit.

She walked into her room. Walking was less painful than standing upright had been, but she had to move carefully, more gliding than walking, because any little jolt meant a release of bolts of pain. Once at her bed, she stayed standing, not sure she could face sitting and then standing again. She did have to lean over to pick up her laptop that she'd left on her bed. She whimpered while she did it.

She set it on top of the chest of drawers and opened it. It took a while to do one-handed—her left hand at that—but she finally managed to find the information about how to get medical care. That reminded her that she had an insurance card somewhere. She fished her wallet out of the fanny pack. It didn't say where she could go. Back to the computer.

Finally, she figured out the closest emergency room that was covered by her insurance. It was called Duniway Memorial Hospital. After a short debate with herself, she called an Uber. Her arm wasn't up to the jostling of a bus. It was quite swollen already. She stood on the front porch waiting, still not trusting her ability to shift from sitting to standing or the other way around without pain. Getting in and out of the car would be bad enough.

The Uber driver was a woman who, when she saw Lenka getting into her car with her arm pressed against her chest, asked, "Are you sure you don't need an ambulance, hon?"

"It's just my arm. It's fine." An ambulance where someone else did all the moving for her and perhaps gave her meds to ease the pain sounded like a dream. However, looking over her insurance information had instilled in her a dread of doing something wrong and having to pay for it. Taking an ambulance when a person didn't need one was one of their examples.

"Okay," the driver said skeptically, "but if you pass out or anything, I'm calling an ambulance."

"I won't." Lenka hoped it was true. It was a lot of pain.

She got through the drive by white-knuckling the door handle with her good hand and holding herself as still as possible. She wanted to weep when they finally arrived. When she had to get out of the car, she did shed some tears. Such a good day, followed by this. And this wasn't just going to go away overnight. It would take time to heal. The thought of this pain continuing filled her with dread.

She joined the line of people checking in, surprised by how many were in need of emergency care at…she had no idea what time it was. She found a clock over the receptionist's desk and saw it was nearly eleven. It was less than an hour ago that she'd walked into the dark house. It felt like it had been all night.

"What is the problem today?" the receptionist asked without looking up. It was the same question Lenka had heard her ask of the two people in front of her. She hadn't heard their answers with them faced away and a separation of about five feet from the end of the line to the desk.

"I think I broke my arm."

"Injured arm. Okay."

Lenka resented that. It was injured, sure, but that made it sound like a bruise or something. This was more than that. In fact, looking at her arm, she saw it was bruised now. The swelling had gotten worse, too. She didn't protest, just went through the process with the receptionist, who told her in the end to go have a seat. "Are you left-handed?"

"No."

The receptionist sighed. "Then you won't be able to do your paperwork. Just take this, and someone will help you with it." She thrust a clipboard at Lenka, who shifted to one side to protect her right arm and took it with her left hand.

"You'll be called for triage soon."

Triage was a word Lenka wasn't familiar with, but she didn't have the energy or fortitude to pull her phone out and look. It was all she could do to stand there, not wanting to go through another vertical change. She was both wired and exhausted, already tired of being in pain. The combination made her stomach churn.

When someone called out something close to her name, she went with him, not bothering to correct him. He asked her to sit in a little room.

"I'd rather not have to sit and stand."

"Is there something wrong with your legs?"

"No. It's just the arm."

He finally looked at it. Her arm had swollen and was black and blue. "Oh, boy. You've done a number here, haven't you? Why didn't you ask for a wheelchair?"

Lenka had no idea how to respond to that. She'd had no idea it was an option, and no one had offered her one. He left the curtained area and came back pushing one.

"Here. Have a seat."

She gingerly lowered herself and hoped she'd get to stay for a long while. He performed an evaluation, then wheeled her back to the waiting room and told her it wouldn't be long. He also filled out her paperwork for her, even though he said it was someone else's job.

The next person to call her name said it right. The voice was also tinged with worry. "Lenka?"

It was Grace. She was dressed in blue scrubs and kneeling in front of Lenka, who must have been spacing out since she'd missed her arrival. "Grace. Hi. Sorry."

"No, no. What are you sorry for? What happened? Never mind. You can tell me in a minute. Let's get you to a room and get you more comfortable."

Grace moved behind her and pushed her wheelchair toward double doors. She held her badge to a scanner that opened the doors and pushed Lenka through.

"We're just going to go into room three. I'll get an IV started to administer meds. A doctor will take a look. She'll almost certainly send you over to radiology for an X-ray to see what needs to be done next. The next step will depend on that result. Sound good?"

"As good as anything can sound right now." Grace was clearly in her element here. She was confident and knowledgeable. Lenka hadn't heard her speak so much since the night she'd picked Lenka up from the airport when, in retrospect, Lenka realized she'd probably been babbling nervously. But Lenka still didn't understand why. What was it about her that had made this confident woman nervous?

"I bet," Grace said with sympathy. She rolled Lenka into the room and set the brake on the wheelchair. "I need to gather a few things, then I'll be right with you."

Lenka watched her go, feeling grateful that she hadn't been told to get up on the bed. The thought of hopping onto that high bed was more than daunting. Grace was back in minutes carrying medical looking things that she sorted onto a light blue sheet laid out on the table.

"How did this happen?"

Lenka didn't want her to feel responsible or anything, but she also didn't want to lie to her. "Um, it was Loki."

Grace turned to her and froze, holding a wipe in one of her gloved hands. She looked pale, which was unusual. Her skin tone was usually a light tan with warm undertones. Not that Lenka spent a lot of time analyzing the color of her skin.

Lenka hurried to explain. "He's okay. He was just under my feet in the hall, and it was dark, so I didn't see him until it was too late. I fell, but he was moving fine."

"Oh, um, I'm glad he's okay, but it's you I'm worried about right now. I'm so sorry."

Lenka shook her head, but even that felt dangerous. She stilled it. "It's not your fault."

"I mean, it kind of is. He's my cat. Why was it dark?" Grace leaned over and examined Lenka's arms. "Any history of opioid addiction? Have you had an IV before?"

"No and no," Lenka said, answering the last questions first. "And it was dark because I thought you were asleep."

Grace looked up, and Lenka noticed her eyes for the first time. They were brown but nearly amber by her pupils, darkening to black around the edges. They were good eyes. "You were trying to not wake me up?"

"Yes. I mean, I know you work hard and need your sleep."

"Goodness, Lenka, you're about the most thoughtful roommate ever, but please turn on a light. Especially with that little monster running around. We can't have this happening again."

Lenka felt chastised. She'd walked in the dark plenty before without breaking an arm. She was considering a response when Grace took her uninjured arm and ran a finger along her forearm. Lenka was surprised to find herself focusing on that when her other arm hurt so much. She watched in fascination as Grace settled on a spot and rubbed it with an alcohol wipe. When the astringent smell hit her, she realized she'd been smelling Grace's shampoo. It was citrusy.

"This'll pinch." Grace poked her with the needle. It stung, but it was brief and nothing on the pain in her arm. Still, it broke her out of the trance she'd been in. Grace moved with confidence and efficiency, attaching a bag to the end of the IV. The pain ebbed almost immediately.

"What is in there?"

"The good stuff," Grace said. "Are you feeling it already?"

"Yes." Lenka sighed with relief. Even that movement didn't make it hurt. Too much.

A woman came through the curtains and started speaking while she held her hand under the sanitizer dispenser and rubbed it in. "Hello. I'm Dr. Reddick. We have an arm injury here?"

Lenka wasn't sure if the question was directed at her or Grace. She flung a questioning look Grace's way.

"Aubrey, this is my, um, roommate, Lenka. And, yes, she tripped over Loki."

Dr. Reddick looked back and forth between them, a grin spreading across her face. "Ah! You must be the exchange student."

Grace had talked about her at work? "Yes, that's me."

"Loki is a menace. Remember that dinner you hosted last year when he pushed the nearly full bottle of wine off the counter?"

Grace had friends over? All of this was shifting Lenka's perception of her. She'd thought of her as a loner, someone who didn't like spending time around people. Maybe it was just Lenka she was trying to avoid. That wasn't hurtful at all.

Grace chuckled, the first time Lenka had heard her laugh. It was a throaty chuckle. Lenka almost felt the rumble. Man, these drugs were good. Grace added a rueful headshake. "At least it didn't cause bodily injury, and the floors were linoleum, so it was easy to clean up. This"—she gestured at Lenka—"is a more serious infraction on his part."

"Okay, well, let's have a look." Dr. Reddick leaned over Lenka's arm and examined it. She asked questions, made her do things that hurt, and pronounced it was likely broken, but they needed X-rays to evaluate and decide what needed to be done.

"Doesn't it just need a cast?" Lenka asked.

"If it's a clean break, that is to say that the broken bone ends are in alignment, then, yes, it's a matter of a cast. Actually, in that case, you'll get a temporary cast and come in for an appointment to have it recast when the swelling goes down in a few days. But there's the possibility it will need to be set. We'll know more after the X-ray."

"What does that mean, to set it?" Medical language wasn't Lenka's strongest suit. She knew all these words but not in the context.

"It means to manipulate the bones so they line up again."

That sounded painful.

Grace placed a hand on her shoulder. "If that needs to be done, you'll be heavily sedated for it."

"Yes, that's right," Dr. Reddick agreed. "Any other questions?"

Lenka numbly shook her head, then stopped abruptly. It didn't hurt her arm, but she was still a little skittish about moving. "No." She was sure there were things she should ask, but she couldn't think of them.

"Well, if you think of any, I'm sure Grace can answer them for you. Or she'll know who to ask, at least." Dr. Reddick winked at Grace and left.

"Wait here for a few minutes while I go send the order for the X-rays. Someone will come wheel you over to radiology shortly." Grace patted her shoulder—thoughtfully not the one attached to the broken arm—and left.

Lenka sat and wondered how she was supposed to do anything besides sit and wait. She supposed it would be possible to stand and walk out, but she certainly couldn't wheel herself anywhere with that arm. And why would she? This was where the IV with its load of pain numbing drugs was.

Some minutes later, she heard voices coming her way. She didn't pay them much mind until they stopped just on the other side of her curtains, and she recognized one of them as Grace.

"Are you sure?" Grace was asking. "Aren't we understaffed?"

"Not only am I sure that you should take care of your exchange student tonight, but I've noticed that your hours have gotten way out of hand, even after we talked about it. Go home with her when she's discharged, and I don't want to see you again for a week."

"What? No. I'm on the schedule the day after tomorrow."

"I know, but you shouldn't be. I can call someone else in tonight if I need to. You shouldn't be the one covering for Liz. You're way over. You have to take some time, or the department will be in for it. Rest up. Take care of…Lenka?"

"Yes, Lenka." Grace sounded resigned. Lenka worried that she would resent her for being the reason she was sent home. While it sounded like she'd been working too much overtime—which sort of explained her absenteeism—it was Lenka being here that seemed to have triggered this suspension. But it was also out of her hands. She couldn't make Grace's boss let her work. It would be what it would be.

"You'll get through. See you in a week. And then, stick to regular time for a while. No more overtime for at least a month after that. Meaning that I don't want to see your face on night shift for at least five weeks. Got it?"

"Got it." Grace sounded beaten down.

There were footsteps leaving, but they were soon lost in the general noise of the emergency room. It was loud in here. The rooms were really like three-sided stalls that all opened into a central area that must have been the nurse's station. There were curtains for privacy, but Lenka had noticed several of them were occupied and still had open curtains. Maybe so the nurses could keep an eye on the inhabitants. Lenka's were pulled. They were mostly a light green with some sort of pattern on them. Squares. Lenka was staring at them and wondering if they were moving or if it was the drugs when the curtains whipped aside, and Grace came in.

She smiled wanly. "How are you doing?"

"Fine, I think." She shrugged. That pain did cut through at that. She winced. "Maybe not fine."

"I mean, you do have a broken arm. You're not expected to be completely fine. When it's set and immobilized, that will help a lot with the pain." That was a relief to hear. Lenka had been worried that this level of pain would continue for days or more. Grace moved behind her and started pushing the wheelchair. "We're off to radiology."

"You're coming with me? I thought it would be someone else."

"Me too." Grace gave a little unamused laugh. "It's usually an orderly, but apparently, you now have exclusive nursing care."

"I'm sorry."

Grace pushed in silence for a moment. Lenka wondered if she was too mad to speak. They'd gone through a set of doors Grace had to use her badge to open and made a couple of turns before Grace spoke. "No, it's me who is sorry. I haven't been a good host. And now you've broken your arm and are the one apologizing to me. You have nothing to be sorry for. It's me and my out of control cat who owe you an apology."

Lenka absorbed that for a minute. She was just about to reply when they stopped at a desk. Grace handed something to the person there. "Lenka Supik for X-rays."

"Wheel her over there." The desk guy pointed to a spot next to a few chairs. "We'll be with you in a moment." That was directed at Lenka. "We'll send her back when we're done." That was for Grace.

"I'm staying with her." He looked surprised and opened his mouth to say something, but Grace spoke first. "I'm here as a friend, not a nurse."

"Gotcha. Okay, then. Have a seat."

When they were settled, Lenka said, "Even if you're not allowed to stay at work, you don't have to stay with me. You could go home and get some sleep. You must be tired. Didn't you work the day shift today?"

"I did. But it's okay. It sounds like I'll be getting plenty of sleep over the next week. Besides, I was planning on staying up all night tonight working anyway."

"Why have you been working so much? Do you have money troubles?" The bag connected to her IV had come with her, hanging from a pole attached to the wheelchair. Lenka figured that was part of why she had a loose tongue.

Grace looked at her, then up at the bag. The corner of her mouth twitched. "I mean, money is always tight, but that is exactly why I decided to host an exchange student. I'd been looking for a roommate and having trouble finding one. Then, I saw an ad. It seemed like a good solution to my problems. With the monthly payment from your exchange program, I'm making ends meet fine. No, I've been working so much because I'm a coward."

"What do you mean?"

Grace put her face in her hands. She scrubbed up and down a few times. "I've been hiding from you."

Lenka reared back, then wished she hadn't as pain shot up her arm. Grace had been avoiding her. "Why? I'm sorry. Should I move out?"

"No! No. I mean, please don't. It's nothing you've done. I…I was expecting a teenager, and I was surprised. Then, I ran my mouth when I picked you up, and that was embarrassing. I also figured you didn't really need me because you're an adult, so I was hiding out at work. The extra money didn't hurt."

"Oh." Maybe the avoidance wasn't personal. That was hopeful. She just wanted Grace around because she wanted to have someone to practice English with at home. That was it. "Well, is it a problem I'm not a teenager?"

"No, not really. But after the embarrassment of the night I picked you up, I just established a pattern of keeping my distance, and even when I wanted to break it, it was hard. Plus, it seems you've found your way. You're out a lot."

"Yeah, well, I really, really need to practice my English. I've been looking for opportunities to do so. Going out means spending time with people I'm forced to speak English with."

"Your English is really good, though. Why do you need so much practice?"

"Lenka Supik?" A woman stood in front of Lenka. "Ready?"

Lenka looked at Grace, wondering if she was coming.

"I'll wait here. No one else is allowed in the X-ray room."

"That's right," the woman said. She started pushing Lenka. "So how did you do this?"

"I tripped over a cat."

"You'd be amazed at how many people that happens to."

CHAPTER NINE

Grace watched as Lenka was wheeled away, leaving her with her thoughts. She didn't think she regretted being candid with her. It was likely the only way forward. They'd be spending a lot of time together this week for sure because Lenka would need help with her newly broken arm and also for the eight months that Lenka would be living with her. She didn't want to keep hiding. Nor did she want things to be awkward. And she did want to be a good host. Not host parent. That ship had sailed when she'd met Lenka at the airport. She could be a host, though. Actually eat meals with Lenka sometimes, hold conversations so she could practice her already excellent English. She could do this.

When Lenka was wheeled back out, Grace stood, ready to take over wheelchair duties. Lenka smiled wanly at her. Man, she was cute. She had a dimple on her left cheek. *Okay, none of that.* Grace might not have been her host parent, but she was her host. Not only that, but the poor woman was in pain. Grace could be a friend, roommate, and if Lenka needed it, guide. But Lenka didn't need her host macking on her, especially if she was like the Polish grandparents Grace had heard about and had a problem with gay people.

"How'd it go?"

"Taking off the hoodie was a nightmare. And one way I had to lay my arm was painful."

"Ah, yes. Sorry about that. Medical treatment isn't always comfortable."

"I imagine it would have been much worse without whatever magic juice is in that bag."

"Indeed."

They were silent for the length of a hall. Then, Lenka asked, "What happens next?"

"The radiologist will look at your X-ray and talk to Dr. Reddick, who will decide what happens next. Aubrey, Dr. Reddick, is an orthopedist, so she's the one who will do whatever needs to be done."

"And Aubrey is a friend of yours? Sorry, Dr. Reddick."

"I don't think she'd mind you calling her Aubrey. And, yes. As she mentioned, she's been over to the house. Although, the incident she referenced with Loki happened at the apartment I lived in before." Loki had been a kitten then and even worse about shoving things over.

"Do you host often?"

Grace really hadn't been doing her job well. She could have introduced Lenka to all sorts of people but had cut her off from that possibility, all because she'd been caught flat-footed that night at the airport. "I don't know about often, but I like to have people over for dinner sometimes on my days off."

"You cook?"

The fact that Lenka didn't even know that was…well, Grace was going to do better. "I do. And I like having people over because then I know it's vegan. When I go to other people's houses, it's more of a gamble." She figured that one of the reasons Lenka had been placed with her was because she was vegetarian. They were fairly well matched in that department. Grace had finally looked over the placement email. She'd also discovered that Lenka enjoyed hiking, which was something Grace liked. It was really a good placement. Aside from the misunderstanding that had undermined it all.

"That makes sense."

Grace used her badge to open the door to the ED, then pushed Lenka back to her room. "I'll just go check with Aubrey. Back in a sec."

Aubrey was sitting at the nurse's station looking at a monitor. Grace looked over her shoulder and saw Lenka's X-rays. That was fast. It hadn't been too busy over there, so it wasn't that surprising. And as far as Grace knew, there hadn't been any other orthopedic patients who'd come into the ED that night. She glanced at the board to confirm. No, she was wrong. Someone else was noted as needing an orthopedic consult.

"Are you skipping Lenka up the line because she's my roommate?"

Aubrey looked up at her and scoffed. "You only think you're special. And roommate? That pink-haired pixie who is exactly your type is your host daughter."

Grace groaned. "Shh. She's right over there."

Aubrey grinned, unrepentant. "Host daughter."

"I've decided that there is absolutely no parent-child relationship here. I'll thank you to respect my wishes in this regard," Grace said with as much dignity as she could muster.

"Yeah, okay, sure. I hear you're being kicked out of here. Serves you right, all the overtime shenanigans you've been pulling."

"Hey. We were understaffed."

"Yeah, okay. Whatever. Anyway, your kid's arm is broken."

Grace groaned. She'd known the arm was broken. "Don't call her my kid."

"And it'll need to be set. I think it'll be external manipulation, but you know how it goes. There's the possibility I'll have to cut. I'm going to have her stay overnight for observation."

"Well, that's not entirely unexpected."

Aubrey gave a short nod. "Let's go tell her."

"Please don't call her my kid in front of her."

"We'll see."

Grace groaned again and followed her back to Lenka's room. She needn't have worried. Aubrey was professional, if a little extra friendly. She explained the procedure and the possibilities, explained that Lenka would stay overnight. Then, she added that if all went well, Grace could take her home around noon.

Lenka shot Grace a look.

Grace answered the unspoken question, "I'll go home to sleep a few hours once your procedure is done, and you're settled, but I'll come back in the morning and hang out with you until they release you. And, yeah, I'll take you home." A little shot of embarrassment rippled through her. She hadn't meant it that way. She was probably the only one who thought it sounded scandalous.

Nope. Aubrey was smirking at her. "I've got to check on another patient. I'll meet you up in pre-op shortly." She smiled reassuringly at Lenka, smirked again at Grace, and left.

"Is there anyone you need to tell about all this? Parents? Boyfriend? I can't imagine you can text left-handed. Or are you left-handed?"

"No." She sounded sad. "Definitely right-handed. I think this is going to make school difficult."

Grace winced sympathetically. "I imagine so. You should ask for accommodations." She leaned back in her chair and crossed her legs at the ankles. "It's something we tell students all the time. If you have a disability—and this counts, even though it's temporary—your school has systems in place to help. For example, they'll have someone else in each of your classes take notes for you."

"That would help. I don't think I can type one-handed fast enough. And there are people I should tell. In fact, my parents are probably awake now. I could call them." She fumbled with the hoodie in her lap.

"Do you need a hand with that?"

Lenka dropped her hand in apparent defeat. "Sure."

Grace leaned forward and pulled the hoodie off Lenka's lap. The phone was heavy in the kangaroo pocket. There was a wallet there, too. She retrieved the phone and handed it to Lenka, who fumbled to unlock it with her left hand, and after several long moments during which Grace's fingers twitched to take it and help, she held it up to her ear. She said something that Grace had difficulty parsing.

She was somehow surprised it wasn't English because Lenka's English was so good. She found herself staring for a few long moments, amazed at Lenka's linguistic abilities. Definitely not because Lenka was cute, even if Aubrey was right about her being Grace's type. When she realized she was staring, she looked away and figured this was a good time to go get a tea. As much as she loved coffee, she had a hard cutoff at two in the afternoon or at midnight if she was working night shift, even though she'd be awake for a while yet.

She felt bad not getting anything for Lenka, but she was potentially going into surgery and couldn't eat or drink anything. As she stood and waited for her tea to steep, she pulled her phone out. Maci would be asleep, being a day shift person, but she'd want this news from Grace before she heard it secondhand tomorrow. She typed out such a long explanation that her tea was strong by the time she removed the bag. That was fine. She was a fan.

She considered changing into street clothes, but the scrubs were comfortable and made her look like she belonged at the hospital. When she returned to Lenka's room, she heard her still talking and paused before parting the curtains. She didn't want to intrude. But she was pretty sure she was speaking French now, even though her mostly forgotten high school French didn't help her to understand. Was it because she was talking to someone new, or did she just flow through different languages?

When Lenka fell silent, Grace went in. Lenka looked cheerier. Her gaze went to the tea in Grace's hand.

"Sorry," Grace said. "I'd offer you something, but you can't eat or drink before your procedure. When did you last eat or drink?" She really should have been doing her job. No one else had come to check, so it was down to her. She did actually have things she was supposed to be doing.

"Dinner, I guess? It was around six. I might have had a drink of water after that?"

"Hang on a sec. I should do some charting and take your vitals again."

Grace went to the nurses' station and grabbed one of the computers on wheels. "Okay. How'd the call with your parents go? Everything okay at home?"

"Yes, sure. They're a little worried about me, but I told them I'd be fine, that I was in good hands." She smiled again. It looked like work.

Grace wanted to live up to being the good hands, so she did her job, taking vitals and charting. She was just finishing up when an orderly came in saying, "Knock-knock. I'm here to take you up to the surgical ward. Ready to go?"

Lenka looked at Grace. "Can she come with me?"

The orderly looked at Grace, too. "Normally—"

"It's okay. It's not normally. I know her. In fact, I can just take her if you want."

He shrugged his indifference. "Go for it."

"Thanks for coming with me," Lenka said. "It's a comfort."

Grace felt the opposite of comfort. She'd have been a lot more comforting if she'd bothered to get to know Lenka in the last two months, but she said, "That's what I'm here for."

❖

"Look. I can lift my arm." Lenka lifted her broken arm to prove it. She was being wheeled out of the procedure room on a gurney and waved the temporary cast in the air.

Grace knew that it was the pain meds talking, but it was still good to see Lenka happy. "Yes, look at you. It's a miracle of modern medicine."

Aubrey had stopped by about ten minutes prior to explain that she'd been able to set the arm externally, and it had gone well. Then, she'd rushed off to visit her next patient.

"Yes," Lenka said, looking at her arm like all her dreams had come true.

Grace fell into step next to the gurney and traveled with her to the room she was staying in. It was semi-private. There were two beds with a curtain that could be drawn between them. The other was empty for now. There was a bustle as Lenka was transferred to the bed, and her nurse came in, introduced herself, and got her settled. And, of course, there was the curious look at Grace that she had gotten used to on this strange night.

"I'm a friend. But I'll get out of your hair for now and come back in the morning."

"It is after visiting hours." The nurse looked Grace up and down. "But we're slow here tonight. If you want to crash in the empty bed, go for it."

Grace looked at Lenka, who was beaming like it was Christmas morning—the drugs were definitely coursing strongly through her system—and accepted with thanks. Lenka might not have cared about Grace being there once the drugs began to clear out, but right now, she clearly wanted company. It was the least Grace could do to make up for not only her cat's behavior but the way she had acted for the last couple of months. Besides, making Lenka look that happy made her feel good.

Chapter Ten

It made total sense to Lenka to have Grace spend the night when the nurse offered. But when her nurse woke her up for a check at four a.m., she wondered what she'd been thinking. She barely knew Grace. Why had she encouraged her to stay?

There was something about her that Lenka found comforting. Maybe just that little bit of familiarity, not to mention she'd been a very competent caregiver.

Lenka slept fitfully for another few hours, looking over at the lump that was Grace every time she shifted. Even if it didn't make sense to want her to stay, she was still glad Grace was there. She still wanted her there for reasons she wasn't clear on. She wasn't in pain. She still had an IV and figured it was still giving her happy juice. She was just having a hard time sleeping in the hospital. There was too much light. There were machines that beeped. People came in and out of the room all the time.

Grace seemed to sleep through it all. Maybe it was because she was used to the atmosphere. Also, she was probably exhausted. While Lenka had slept in until ten that morning—or the previous morning now—Grace had been up for work at six, not to mention that she'd been working all that overtime to get away from home.

That was a blow to Lenka's ego. Sort of. She did kind of get where Grace was coming from about her embarrassment. And she was glad to have the explanation.

But now what? Were they suddenly going to become besties? It did seem they'd be spending a lot of time together this week. Grace because she'd been kicked out of her sanctuary, and Lenka because she was probably going to need a few days before facing the world. She felt…weird. There wasn't much pain, but she was wary about it coming back. She was extremely tired. She felt off-kilter. Maybe some of it was meds, maybe some was shock. She didn't know. But what she wanted most in the world was to be home. Not at Grace's house, which was fine, but in a place that really felt like home. Where it felt cozy, safe, and familiar. Where was that mystical place now?

It wasn't in Louny at her parents' house. She'd felt like she'd tried to put on clothes that were too small there. It wasn't the apartment in Prague where she'd lived for six years of work and then school. That had felt like home, but her room belonged to someone else now. There was no well-known bed with her own comforter and pillows where she knew the way to get the most comfort, no posters she'd chosen for the walls, no smell of her roommate cooking something to share wafting down the hall. It couldn't be in New York. She'd never even been there.

It was maybe her grand-mere's house in France. That place had always felt like home, mostly because it meant she was near Grand-mere. But France was far away right now.

She felt adrift.

It was probably just her injury making her feel that way. She looked at Grace once more and wondered at wanting her there. Maybe the adrift feeling was because she was coming to terms with having felt rejected. But why would that matter so much? They were just roommates. Right?

She shifted, and her IV pinched her arm, drawing her attention. Maybe it was the drugs. She sighed. Whatever it was, she didn't like it.

During shift change, when her night nurse came in and introduced her to her day nurse, Grace finally stirred. Lenka had only been wheeled into the room around two a.m. and now it was a little after seven. Five hours wasn't a lot of sleep, but it was at least two more hours than Lenka had gotten. Still, she tried not to be judgey.

"Hi, Lenka," the day nurse said. "How are you feeling this morning?"

"Fine. Just a little tired."

"I bet."

Grace sat up and stretched, catching everyone's attention.

"Grace? What are you doing up here?"

"Oh, hi, Tess." Grace yawned. "Just keeping my, um, roommate company."

Roommate. Yes, that's what they were to each other. Lenka liked that better than exchange daughter, for sure.

Tess looked between them. "I see." The tone seemed to indicate that she thought they were more than roommates.

Was Grace queer?

She stood and stretched. "How are you doing this morning, Lenka? Did you get any sleep?"

"Some," Lenka hedged.

"Well," Tess said, "let's do what we can to get you out of here as soon as possible so you can go sleep in your own bed. At Grace's."

"Tess, have you heard that I am hosting an exchange student? Lenka is from the Czech Republic. She's here for school."

Tess's face cleared. "Oh! I see. How did you break your arm?"

While she told Tess the story and they went over what to expect from the day, Lenka thought about Tess's reaction. Had the two of them dated? Were they dating now? Grace didn't act like they were, but Tess had seemed upset about the idea of Lenka and Grace being more. Curious and curiouser.

Another nurse came bursting through the door. "Grace, you're here."

"Good morning, Maci," Grace said, sounding resigned. "Maci, this is Lenka. Lenka, this is my friend Maci who should be down in the ED right now."

Maci waved that off. "I have a few minutes, and I wanted to meet the infamous Lenka. Oh, hi, Tess." She'd sounded excited until she got to the Tess part. Then, she sounded…maybe a little annoyed?

"Maci," Tess said coolly.

"I hear you tripped over Loki last night. He's such a little menace," Maci said with a great deal of affection.

"I need to go check on my other patients. I'll be back with your meds in a bit, Lenka." Tess left.

"How are you doing? How are you liking Portland?" Maci asked like she was settling in for a chat. Lenka would have welcomed that at any other time, but right now, it felt a little overwhelming.

"Maci, leave poor Lenka alone. I'll tell you what. How about you come over for dinner in a few days when she's feeling better? You can chat then. For now, go back to work, slacker." Grace said it with a great deal of affection, so Lenka was pretty sure these two were particular friends.

"I've really enjoyed Portland. I look forward to talking with you when the warden here allows it," Lenka said with a smile to show she didn't mean it. And she didn't. She was grateful to Grace for running interference.

"Okay, okay," Maci said, "I'll go. It was nice to meet you, Lenka, finally, and I look forward to dinner when you're up for it." She also bustled out of the room, leaving Lenka and Grace alone.

"I'm sorry I kept you out of your bed last night," Lenka said.

"Please. Because you tripped over my cat, I actually got a little sleep. I should be thanking you."

"You're right. You'd have been working all night if not for me. You're welcome."

Someone in scrubs came in carrying a tray. "Breakfast," she said by way of explanation and left again.

Lenka lifted the tray and looked in disappointment at the watery eggs, sausage, floppy looking toast, and anemic fruit mix. "Well."

"I know. Hospital food. It's not exactly the height of cuisine. But they do have pudding and Popsicles if either of those is more appealing." She leaned in as if she was telling a secret. "And I know where they keep them." She straightened back up. "Like Tess said, you will have to eat something and prove you can keep it down before they let you go home."

"I can eat a piece of toast." But Lenka doubted it even as she said it. "Actually, pudding sounds good. Chocolate?"

Grace smiled at her. "I'm sure that can be arranged. I'll be right back."

Lenka rested her head against the rubbery hospital pillow. Grace's house might not feel like home, but it was better than this. She was ready to get out of here. She'd even eat the limp toast if she had to. She closed her eyes and willed herself to rest a little.

When she heard the voices in the hall, she at first thought she'd dozed off. But when she opened her eyes, she was sure she was awake, but the voices—was that… No, it wasn't Czech, but it was close. Polish. They weren't the same language, not at all, but there were similarities, and with her ear for languages, she could understand most of what was being said. It sounded like music to her ears after the deluge of English for the last seven or so weeks. But what he was saying was troubling. He was trying to explain that his wife was having…pain in a new place? Yes. She was sure.

Tess had said that she should be moving around. She'd yet to be brave enough to get up, even though her need to pee was getting to the point where she'd have to. It was the conversation in the hall that gave her the push to actually rise. The head of her bed was at an angle, so she was practically sitting up already. She swung her legs off and tentatively scooted. Her feet were clad in socks with grippers that the hospital had provided. With her good hand braced on the bed and her casted arm held close to her chest, she pushed to standing. It was okay.

She swayed a little. Maybe not okay. She pushed down on the bed with her good hand to stabilize. Back to okay.

The voices continued in the hall, speaking past each other. She heard the English speaker say, "I'm sorry. We're going to have to wait for a translator. Are you speaking Russian?"

It was going to take a while if they didn't even know the correct language. The Polish speaker must have understood that much, though. He said, "No. Polski." He continued on in full Polish, explaining that it was in the chart.

Well, it must have been. They had to have had a translator at some point to get this far, hadn't they? He sounded worried and exasperated. Lenka took a step. Okay. It was okay. Tess had removed her IV, so she didn't have to haul the stand with her. Although, it might have been good to have something to hold on to. She took another step and another, and pretty soon was trailing her good hand along the wall that separated her room from the bathroom, and she was in the hall.

"Do you need something?" It was Tess. She'd been the one talking to the Polish speaker.

"I might be able to help." She turned to the man and spoke her best Polish. It wasn't good—she was sure it was heavily accented—but his face lit up, so it must have been passible. He grabbed her arm, thankfully her good one, and started speaking quickly. She asked him to slow down.

He took a breath and started again, complying with her request. This time, Lenka got it. "He's saying that his wife's left side is painful. And maybe tender to the touch? Yes, I think so. But apparently, her original pain was higher."

"Oh. Oh! Thank you. Can you come with me? Are you up for walking?" Tess looked her up and down.

"I am. I think."

"I'll help." It was Grace back with two puddings. "Just let me set these down. Lenka can hold on to me if she needs a little support."

"If you could come talk to his wife with me, it would help so much," Tess said to Lenka.

Lenka thought they'd already decided that, but maybe she'd missed something. "I'm happy to."

Grace came back out of the room empty-handed and held her arm out for Lenka to grasp. She probably didn't need it, but it gave her some confidence. They went to a room two doors down.

A woman lay in the bed clutching her side and looking pained. She asked her husband if he'd found help, and he indicated Lenka. She introduced herself in Polish and offered to translate as much as she was able. The woman looked relieved and started explaining what was going on. Lenka had to ask her to slow down, as she had her husband, but eventually, she was able to tell Tess what was going on. She had to work around words she wasn't sure of, but eventually, the idea got across.

"I need to call the doctor. Would you be willing to translate when he gets here again?" Tess asked.

"Sure. But I need to use the bathroom."

Grace gave a little snort. "Talk about putting others first. I'll take you back to your room for the bathroom and some pudding. Tess, come get us when the doctor gets here, okay?"

"Okay. Thanks, Grace. And you, too, Lenka."

She didn't begrudge the thanks to Grace, but it was a little odd that she was the afterthought when she was the one translating, but oh well. It was sort of amusing. The husband thanked her profusely, making up for it, before he turned worriedly back to his wife.

"That was pretty impressive," Grace said as they went down the hall. "You should get a job as a translator for the hospital."

Lenka was amused. "You know I'm going to school to be a translator, right?"

"Oh. Right. I guess I'd kind of forgotten. How many languages do you speak?"

"Well? Three. Czech, English, and French."

"If that back there wasn't speaking Polish, well, I don't know what is."

Lenka snorted at that. "That was extremely poor Polish. It's just lucky there are similarities with Czech. I can speak a few languages at that level. Russian and German in addition to Polish."

"Wow. That's amazing. My grandma on my mom's side was Italian and was always disappointed that no one in my generation spoke it. I know a tiny bit of French from high school and a few words of Spanish, mostly from TV and restaurants, and that's about it."

"I know a little Spanish if you want to practice together."

"Of course you do." Grace sounded amused. "Will you be okay in there by yourself?"

They were standing outside the door of the bathroom. Lenka didn't really need help. It hadn't stopped her from taking Grace's arm on the way back just for comfort, but she could stand and even walk on her own two feet. "I'll be fine." She squeezed Grace's arm in thanks and let go.

While she was awkwardly washing her left hand one-handed—and it needed it, she wasn't used to wiping with the left—she realized she hadn't yet called Mackenzie to tell her about her broken arm. She wondered if she had time before the doctor got there. Then, she wondered if Mackenzie was even up yet. Theater hours and all.

"You okay in there?" Grace called.

Lenka opened the door. "Yeah. Just exploring the limits of the capabilities of my left hand."

Grace winced sympathetically. "It's always the dominant arm, isn't it?"

Lenka wouldn't know, but she nodded anyway. "I need to call my girlfriend."

Grace looked surprised. "Okay. Do you want me to leave? Give you some privacy?"

"No, no. It's fine. I was just saying it aloud so I'd remember. I should have at least texted her or something, but at least this way, she'll know I'm okay. I'll video chat her. If she's up."

Grace looked at the clock hanging on the wall. "It is still early."

"Not in New York. But Mackenzie is a night owl. It goes with being an actor."

"Your girlfriend is an actor in New York? How'd that come about? Sorry." Grace waved her hands. "You don't have to answer that. I'll let you call her. Eat some of that pudding, too."

"I don't mind telling you but maybe later. I want to try her before the doctor comes."

"Of course. I'll just..." Grace pointed out the door.

Lenka watched her go, wanting to call her back. She was probably developing a crisis attachment to her. Grace wouldn't want her to be all clingy. She'd labeled them roommates, and that was the relationship they'd have. She wasn't Lenka's mom, even if she was her host mom. It was still funny.

Mackenzie picked up but sounded sleepy. "'Lo? It's early. What's up, babe?"

Lenka lifted her temporary cast that ran from just below her fingers to above her elbow. Because of where the break was, Aubrey had set it so that Lenka's palm faced up. It was extremely awkward.

Mackenzie's eyes widened. "Baby! What happened? Are you okay?"

"Okay enough. I tripped on Loki last night."

"That cat? This is exactly why I don't want pets."

"You don't want pets?" That was news to Lenka. Mackenzie had waxed poetic about the cat she'd had as a child.

"No. Too much work. Too stinky. And look at this. Look what that cat did to you."

Lenka felt the need to defend him. "I mean, it was dark. I should have turned on a light."

"How long do you have to wear the cast?" Mackenzie blew right past that explanation. "Will you have it off by Christmas for my visit?"

"Honestly, I'm not sure. I think someone said, but I don't remember. Six weeks? If that's right, then, yes. It should come off in early December."

Mackenzie's eyes darkened. "Good. Because I've got designs on your body that involve full use of your hands."

Lenka's stomach tightened. Mackenzie's visit couldn't come soon enough.

"Sorry to interrupt, but Tess is asking for us." Grace's head was through the door.

"Who's that?" Mackenzie asked.

"Grace. I need to go, zlatíčko. I'm translating for another patient." It sort of felt good to be the one who had to run off for a change.

"Of course you are. Do-gooder." But Mackenzie's tone was affectionate. Mostly.

CHAPTER ELEVEN

Grace was blown away by Lenka. It was like some sort of rock star was living in her house. She could speak so many languages, was volunteering her time to translate while in the hospital with a broken arm, and somehow had a girlfriend who was an actress in New York. Grace felt out of her league next to her. She could only speak one language, and she'd never left the west coast. If anyone was supposed to be a mentor, it should have been Lenka.

Grace watched her navigate the translations between patient and doctor with humor and ease. The doctor was able to set a course of action and specifically said it was good it was caught right away. Lenka was a freaking hero.

Also, it was nice to know that she didn't have to worry about Lenka being homophobic. Unless she was one of those people who called their friends who were women girlfriends. But Grace was pretty sure that wasn't the case. There was an inflection there. And why would she need to know right away about the broken arm if she was just a friend? No, Grace was pretty sure.

Lenka didn't hold her arm on the journey back to her room, and Grace felt a little sad about it. It had made her feel useful; that was all. "Seriously, you should apply to be a translator here. We have a couple on staff, and with all the languages you speak, you'd be like a multipurpose tool."

Lenka smiled, perhaps at being called a tool. It wasn't exactly flattering now that Grace played it back in her head. "I'd like to, but I'm not allowed to work while I'm here." She paused. "Volunteering is allowed and even encouraged. Do you think I could volunteer as a translator? That would be awesome for both the practice and in terms of doing something useful. I've done a couple of one day volunteering things, but something ongoing like that would be really great."

"I'm sure it's possible. We have all sorts of volunteers. I actually know the volunteer coordinator. I can ask."

"Will you? That would be great." Lenka looked like all her dreams had come true. She was something else.

Grace was glad she was finally getting to know her. She was a remarkable woman. "Absolutely. Now. Let's do what we can to get you out of here. Did you eat that pudding?"

One pudding consumed, a few checks of vitals and fingers, and one doctor's visit later, Lenka was released. It was noon, which was fast, considering hospital bureaucracy. At home, Loki meowed his displeasure at both of them disappearing for the night and twined through their legs.

"Loki!" Grace tried to shoo him away. "Haven't you learned your lesson?"

But Lenka just laughed tiredly. "Clearly, it's the humans who will have to learn to be careful, not him." She yawned. "I think I'll take a nap."

"That's a good plan. I'm going to shower, then do the same. I'm exhausted, and I didn't even break my arm."

Lenka gave a dutiful chuckle and started down the hall.

Grace deposited her pain meds on the counter in the kitchen and filled Loki's bowl. She got out a trash bag and dug up a large rubber band from the junk drawer. She left those in Lenka's bathroom in case she wanted a shower.

After her own shower and nap, Grace felt much more human. Loki was curled up in the curve of her knee and didn't bother to move when she slipped out of bed. He did raise his head to regard her and judge her poor life choices when she opened the curtains she'd pulled for the nap.

"I'm sure you'll get over it," Grace told him.

He shifted and settled with his head twisted so he was lying on it. Cats.

Grace padded down the hall and saw that Lenka's door was still closed. It was nearly time for her next dose of pain meds. If she missed it, she might wake up in a lot of pain. Grace stood outside her door and dithered. She finally decided to give her another half hour before waking her.

She used the time to get started on dinner. It had been so long since she'd really cooked that she had to take stock of what was on hand. She finally decided on a butternut squash soup with seasoned pepitas on top.

She had the squash baking in the oven and the onion and garlic sauteed and simmering in the broth when she decided she couldn't put it off any longer. She got a glass of water and tipped out one of the pills before going to knock on Lenka's door.

There was no answer. She didn't want to invade her privacy, but it was important that she keep the pain at bay. If it got away from her, it could be difficult to get it back under control. Grace knocked one more time, then slowly opened the door, calling, "Lenka?"

No answer. She pushed the door open farther and saw Lenka on her back, cast across her stomach, sound asleep. She looked so peaceful that it broke Grace's heart to wake her, but needs must. She shook her shoulder, the left one, and called her name again.

Finally, Lenka stirred, then her eyes flew open.

"Hi. Sorry," Grace hurried to say. "It's just that it's time for your meds. How do you feel?"

"I don't know yet. Okay, I think. What smells so good?" Lenka's hair was flat on one side and stuck up oddly. It was endearing.

Grace grinned. "Dinner. Here. Let me help you sit up so you can take your pill, okay?" She set the water down and helped lever Lenka up to sitting. Not that she needed to do much work. Lenka seemed to be moving carefully but ably. "How's your pain?"

"Not bad. Do I really need to take that? I don't want to get addicted." The corner of her mouth went up, apparently to show she wasn't too concerned.

"I would. And another before you go to bed. If you don't wake up in the middle of the night in pain, then I'd say you're good to skip taking more if you want. Are they making you feel funky?"

"I couldn't really tell you. I've basically either been seriously sleep-deprived, asleep, or both since I started taking them." She took a drink, tilted her head back, and popped the pill in her mouth.

"Oh, so you're one of those."

"One of what?" Lenka looked confused.

"A water first pill taker."

"Oh. Yeah. Is there another way?"

"Some people, including me, put the pill in first, then take a drink."

Lenka wrinkled her pert nose. "Doesn't the pill start dissolving on your tongue then?"

"It makes you feel alive." Grace grinned. "No, I don't know. It's just how you learn, I guess. I've just noticed the difference as a nurse. The people who are really hard-core are those who swallow pills dry." She gave a performative little shudder.

Lenka nodded seriously. "They're probably sociopaths or something."

"Like black coffee drinkers."

"Exactly."

They grinned at each other for a moment. Grace broke the eye contact first. "I should get back to the kitchen and make sure nothing is boiling over. The soup should be ready in half an hour or so if you want to join me for dinner." Loki sauntered into the room and jumped up on the bed. He checked in with Grace, and after she stroked his little head, he curled up between Lenka's legs. "Traitor," Grace told him. "Although, you should be sucking up after what you did to poor Lenka."

Lenka patted his back. "It's okay, little guy. You didn't mean anything by it."

“You’re letting him off too easy.” But Grace scratched his head even as she said it. “So, yeah. Dinner in thirty. Ish.” She felt a little shy about saying it again. They’d never shared a meal in the time Lenka had lived there, but she hoped she’d join her.

“I’ll be out. Unless I fall asleep again, but if I do, please come wake me up. I am hungry, and it smells great.”

“Will do.” Grace was sporting a little smile as she walked back to the kitchen.

[illegible]

Chapter Twelve

Lenka had considered not going to class today. Only one day of recovery from the broken arm and weird sleep had seemed like maybe not enough. However, she enjoyed her classes and didn't want to miss anything. She was glad they were over now because she was done in. Coming home to find that Grace had dinner nearly ready had been so welcome, she'd almost wept.

"How'd your classes go today?" Grace asked once they'd settled at the table. She'd made a stir-fry tonight. The soup the night before had been fantastic, and the stir-fry smelled like it would be just as good.

"Okay. I had to ask people to take notes, but I talked to the accommodations office before my first class, and they said they should have things set up for me by Wednesday." She stifled a yawn.

"I imagine you're exhausted." Grace gave her a sympathetic look.

Lenka appreciated the sympathy, but she was already tired of needing to be on the end of those looks. She wanted to be normal again. On the other hand, she had to admit she appreciated the change in her homelife. She enjoyed Grace's presence and attention. She picked up the fork rather than the chopsticks that Grace had left by her plate. She could use chopsticks with her right hand, but that seemed way too complicated with her left. It had been very thoughtful of Grace to offer the choice. "This smells great. And, yeah, pretty tired. I think I'll go to bed early tonight."

"And how's the pain?"

Lenka had chosen to switch to acetaminophen that morning. She was also taking something once a day that was supposed to help with the swelling and also provide some pain relief. She could feel her arm for sure, but it was manageable. She hadn't been sure she'd have been able to stay awake and focused if she'd taken the oxy she'd been sent home with. It made her very sleepy. But that was good because she'd slept about fourteen hours between coming home from the hospital until this morning. Still, she'd felt foggy for a few hours this morning, even when it had been about ten hours since she'd last taken the oxy.

"Fine. Minor." She took her first bite of the tofu and broccoli concoction. She nearly moaned with delight. It was so good. Spicy and umami.

"That's good." Grace was looking at her oddly.

Lenka wondered why. Maybe the moan hadn't been nearly but actual. She mentally shrugged it off. So what if it had been? The stir-fry was that good. In fact, she should say so. She jabbed her fork in the direction of her plate and said, "This is really good." As she meticulously forked up her next bite, she asked, "What have you been up to with your copious free time, aside from cooking fabulous meals?"

Grace grinned, presumably at the compliment. She took a bite of her own. She was using chopsticks like a person who had the advantage of her dominant hand. "I got in touch with the volunteer coordinator at Memorial. Her name is Carissa, by the way. I told her all about you and your language prowess. At first, she said she'd have to check with HR, but she called back super excited. There's a serious need, and they'd love to have you. I'll text you Carissa's contact info. There's some paperwork and stuff, but she's excited to hear from you when you feel up to it. She knows about your arm and that it may be a bit before you're ready to take on more than recovery and school at the same time."

"Oh no. I'll get in touch with her tomorrow. I'm really excited. I'd do it tonight except I imagine she works regular office hours?" This was perfect. Lenka would get some real translating experience and be able to help people. It was something she'd wanted since she'd first seen houseless people and been told to ignore them. It wasn't helping them directly, but it was something she could do to help people in general with the skills she had.

Grace paused with her chopsticks halfway to her mouth, looking surprised at Lenka's enthusiasm. Lenka started to feel a little self-conscious, like she'd been too overboard, but Grace smiled big. "That's great. I'm excited for you. Just...maybe remember you'll likely need extra rest for a while." She held up her chopstick-free hand. "Sorry. It's the nurse in me. Handing out unasked for advice. Ignore me."

Lenka was touched she cared. "No, please. I appreciate it. And I appreciate you cooking for me. This really is fantastic. Thanks."

"No problem. I should have been cooking from the start. I'm supposed to be the host here."

Lenka waved that away with her fork. "Nah. We're roommates, right?"

Grace grinned. "Right. With my time off, I was thinking of hosting a small dinner party. I don't want to overtax you, but if you felt like you'd be up for it, maybe Thursday night? I want Maci to come, and that's one of her days off this week."

"Sure, I like meeting new people, and I'm always up for more practice."

They chatted more about their days before Lenka regretfully excused herself to go do homework. "But I could do the dishes first."

Grace cocked her head, raised her eyebrows, and ducked her chin, the picture of skeptical.

"Right." Lenka looked at her arm. "I guess I really can't."

"It's fine." Grace waved her off. "I've got all sorts of time this week."

Lenka didn't get much work done before she was too sleepy to go on. It was okay. She only had the one class on Tuesday, so she could do a lot tomorrow. She reflected as she brushed her teeth that while the broken arm was clearly a horrible thing to have happened, the result—a newly developing relationship with Grace—was quite the silver lining. It wasn't until she was almost asleep that she realized she hadn't spoken to Mackenzie since her release from the hospital. Well, she'd been drugged and then busy. She'd put it on her growing to-do list for tomorrow.

CHAPTER THIRTEEN

"Can I help at all?"

Grace jumped and spun around, still holding the wooden spoon she'd been stirring the dahl with.

"Sorry to sneak up on you," Lenka said, but a smile played around the corners of her mouth. She was clearly amused at Grace's out of proportion reaction. And she had reason to be. Grace had known she was home. Until about half an hour ago, they'd been in the living room together. Lenka had been doing homework. Grace had been alternating between reading and messing around on her phone.

When Grace had needed to start dinner for their guests, she'd regretfully dislodged Loki from her lap and gone to the kitchen. Before she'd even made it out of the room, he'd resettled next to Lenka. So, yeah, she'd definitely known Lenka was there.

Grace clicked the volume button on the Bluetooth speaker. The music must have covered Lenka's approach. She looked at her arm. "I don't know. Can you?"

Lenka looked down. She sighed. "I just feel like an invalid. That's a weird word. Even if you're bedridden, no one should be not valid."

Lenka had been sharing her linguistic insights all week. They had eaten dinner together every evening, getting to know each another better. Grace had only become more impressed with Lenka's faculty with languages. These little observations about a language that wasn't her first or even second were amazing. "You are very valid. You just need a little extra care right now. Besides, isn't your homework taking about twice as long?"

Lenka shrugged. "It's not so bad. The accommodation people set me up with someone to type for me. I've been recording my essays and sending them off to be transcribed. It might even be a little easier."

"That's good. I had no idea they'd do quite so much."

"I'm not sure how I'd manage without the help. But anyway, I can at least set the table or something?"

"Sure, if you'd like." If helping made Lenka feel like she wasn't an invalid, Grace wasn't going to stand in her way. Except, she still wasn't letting her do the dishes. Lenka had come out on Wednesday with the trash bag she was using to cover her cast strapped over her arm saying she'd wash the dishes. Grace hadn't let her. Even if it hadn't been her cat who'd caused the injury, it was so much easier for her to do the dishes. But table setting seemed fine. And Grace admired her spirit for wanting to help.

Lenka moved to the cupboard. "How many people are coming?"

"Six, including us. It's Maci, Carissa, Aubrey, and Greg. Greg is Maci's boyfriend."

"No Tess?" Lenka's tone was knowing.

"No." Grace chuckled. "I try to keep her and Maci separate."

Over Tuesday's dinner, the story of Grace and Tess going on a few dates had come out after Lenka had delicately asked if there was some grudge between Tess and Maci. There was. Tess blamed Maci for Grace not wanting to continue to date. Maci was annoyed by Tess's continued mooning over Grace. Grace wasn't a fan of that, either, to be honest, but she figured Tess would get over it, and they could go back to being friends like before their ill-fated attempt to date. She liked Tess. As a friend. As a romantic interest, she just didn't feel it.

In return for that story, Lenka had shared the story of how she and Mackenzie had met. It sounded very romantic, meeting on a train while traveling through Europe. Grace was looking forward to meeting Mackenzie when she came to visit over Christmas. She sounded adventurous.

While Grace continued to cook, Lenka shuttled the dishes and cutlery to the table in small trips so she could manage one-handed. Grace filled her in a little more on the company.

"Maci was supposed to be my roommate before she and Greg decided to move in together. That's how I ended up volunteering to host."

"Why didn't you just find another roommate?"

That led to Grace explaining about the roommate hunt. They were both in stitches over some of the wild things potential roommates had said.

Between giggles, Lenka said, "Is that why there's the rule about the heat and the window?"

"That's why there are most of the rules on that sheet," Grace said. "I might have gotten a little carried away after some of those interviews. The last one was a man who wanted to be naked all the time."

They were still laughing about that encounter when Grace suddenly noticed Maci in the kitchen doorway. She sported a big smile and a bottle of wine. Greg grinned over her shoulder.

"You two sound like you're having way too much fun in here," Maci said. "Or maybe we need to catch up." She went to the drawer with the corkscrew and started working on the cork.

"No catching up. We've yet to have a drink," Grace said. She had been having fun with Lenka. So much fun that it occurred to her that it would have been nice to have met her in a different way, when Lenka didn't have a girlfriend. She squashed the thought. "But I won't say no when you get that thing open."

Greg retrieved wineglasses for them and lined them up on the kitchen island. While Maci was pouring, Carissa and Aubrey showed up. "It smells wonderful in here, Grace," Aubrey said.

"As always." Carissa slid a plate of cookies onto the other end of the island.

Greg retrieved a couple more glasses. Maci continued pouring. "We're going to kill this bottle fast." She paused. "Wait. I suppose I should ask if you're a wine drinker, Lenka. I know the rest are." She frowned a little. "And if you're drinking wine this evening. Are you still on the oxy?"

"No, no pain meds anymore. And I'd love a glass," Lenka said.

"How is your arm?" Aubrey asked. "No pain at all?"

"Only mild aching. It's no big deal."

"But you are still taking the anti-inflammatory, right?" Aubrey accepted a wineglass even as she grilled Lenka.

"Oh, yes. That's the once a day one, right? Yes. I am."

Aubrey relaxed. "That's good. That's the important one. It is also a bit of a pain reliever."

"Okay, people, this is a social gathering, not a checkup," Grace said. Lenka wanted to be treated like a person rather than a patient. Not that patients weren't people, but it was a different relationship than they should have with a person in a social gathering. "Tell me an interesting story from work this week. I'm in withdrawal."

Maci was off, talking about two people who'd come in injured separately. One had a knife wound that they'd insisted was a slip of a kitchen knife, even though that would have been practically impossible. It was clearly a defensive wound on the arm. The other looked like they'd been in a fight but said they'd fallen down some stairs. When Maci was treating the one who looked like they'd been in a fight, the knife wound patient had come barging in, yelling about killing the other one. Turns out they'd been fighting and were brought in separately. They didn't know one another was there until the knife wound guy heard the other one's voice.

"Luckily, Sam was walking by and was able to restrain the knife guy before anyone got hurt. Any more, at least." Maci held up her glass. "To interesting days."

"Speaking of interesting days, you guys aren't going to believe this, but someone came in and asked for a book this week." Greg was a librarian. Sometimes, he did have interesting stories. Working with the public in any capacity often meant notable interactions, although it was true that really exciting stuff did seem to happen less in his workplace.

Maci playfully slapped his arm. "You've been holding out on me. Why haven't I heard this before?"

They all laughed.

"Time to eat," Grace said. "Everyone grab a dish." There weren't actually dishes for everyone to carry over, but most ended up with something to carry. When Lenka went to grab the flatbread, Grace shooed her. "You're already carrying your wineglass. That means your hands are full."

Lenka put her wineglass between her cast and her torso and raised an eyebrow. "I am a woman of many talents."

"I'm sure you are." Grace tried to not let her mind stray. While Lenka was cute and she'd been very much enjoying getting to know her this week, she had a girlfriend, was only here for eight more months, and no one was supposed to date their exchange student. If she had been a regular roommate and single, that would have been a different story. As it was, they were becoming good friends, and Grace didn't need to mess it up by thinking about her in any other way. "But I've got this. Go sit down."

"Yes, ma'am."

Grace looked up to find Maci's eyes on her. Grace shook her head and shrugged a little, friend shorthand for, nothing to see here.

After they passed dishes and started eating, Carissa said, "Thanks for getting that paperwork back so quickly, Lenka. I think you can start as early as next week if you feel ready."

"I'm ready," Lenka said quickly. "That's perfect."

"What's happening?" Greg asked. "I thought I was finally getting company in the not working at Memorial department, but you're going to be working there, too?"

Lenka smiled. "Sorry to let you down, but, yes. I'm going to volunteer as a translator. I'll do a couple of shifts a week at the hospital and be on call other times."

That led into a conversation about which languages Lenka spoke. The others chimed in with their language knowledge or lack thereof. Grace was surprised to learn that Greg spoke some Russian. His grandmother was Russian, and there were certain phrases that were still used in the family. He and Lenka had a brief and apparently hilarious conversation.

The conversation flowed naturally, and dinner flowed into dessert and another bottle of wine. Finally, Carissa called it. "As the only one with a regular Monday through Friday job at the table, I have to work tomorrow. Ready to go home, honey?"

Aubrey took her hand. "With you? Always."

There were groans around the table at their sappiness, but it was the impetus needed to get people moving. Maci was working Friday as well. Greg, too, but his shift didn't start until afternoon. After the flurry of good-byes, Grace and Lenka were alone again.

"Thank you," Lenka said.

"You're welcome?" Grace wasn't sure exactly what she was being thanked for.

"For introducing me to your friends. It was very fun. When my arm is out of the cast, I could do the cooking for another get-together. Maybe even invite some of my exchange student friends." She looked around. "If you think there's room."

Grace's kitchen table was big. It was the one nice piece of furniture in the house. Old but nice. Maybe it was better described as having character. It was a robust, farmhouse-style table with multiple ways of lengthening it. It had various scratches and dents that gave proof of its use. She'd inherited it from the same grandmother who'd given her down payment money in her will. Grace loved it so much that she'd lived with it crammed into her studio apartment before she'd gotten the house. It fit much better here.

Grace had grown up sitting around this same table with interesting groups of people, mostly family but not infrequently, new friends Grandma had made. Out of her grandchildren, Grandma had apparently recognized Grace as her most kindred spirit in this regard, as she'd left the table to her. All of them had gotten some money for down payments, or if they already had houses, instructions to take elaborate vacations. Sometimes, Grace wished it had been an option to vacation rather than take on the responsibilities of a house. She wasn't that great at homeownership. She needed a roommate to make it work, could barely furnish it, and that yard was still quite the mess. Maybe she'd get to it in the spring.

Anyway, with squishing in and leaves, the table could fit up to a dozen. "Absolutely. But we don't have to wait until your arm heals to have your friends over. Let's set something up."

Lenka's eyes danced, and she looked like she wanted to hug her. Grace felt warm and gooey. It wasn't just about making Lenka happy. No. She'd had a lovely evening with her friends. That was all, nothing more. She certainly wasn't feeling like making Lenka happy was a new goal in life. It was fine. Everything was fine.

CHAPTER FOURTEEN

Ready for the cook-a-thon?" Grace asked when Lenka walked into the kitchen at eight a.m. on Black Friday. Grace was leaning against the counter with a coffee mug in hand. She was wearing jeans that hugged her curves and a loose T-shirt. She looked welcoming and beautiful in a casual way. Cozy. She was the picture of cozy.

If media was to be believed, Lenka had expected to spend this day out fighting hordes of shoppers. She'd been glad that wasn't how it was going to go. She wasn't a huge shopper. What they were doing instead was having a second Thanksgiving. Grace had had to work yesterday, so today, she was hosting a Friendsgiving for an assortment of people ranging from others who'd had to work the day before to exchange students looking to maximize their American holiday experience to people who wanted a fun day to clear out the struggles of celebrations with family the day prior. About a dozen people were coming, making one of the larger dinner parties they'd cohosted.

"Ready and willing." Lenka was down to a below-the-elbow cast that made life much easier all around. She was able to write and type, so she'd said good-bye to her accommodations at school, and she was able to help with cooking, at least some. Which was good because the two of them had gotten into a habit of hosting dinner parties regularly. It was one of Lenka's favorite things about the new normal. The other was the time they spent together cooking, eating, watching TV, all of it was good.

They were cooking vegan spins on traditional Thanksgiving dishes. Nothing took as long as a turkey to cook, but they were making a lot of things, so it would still take a lot of time. Guests were due to arrive at one. Earlier that week, they'd come up with a battle plan, so Lenka knew her first duty was pies. They'd gone the easy route with store-bought pie shells. Lenka would have been happy to do crusts, as she'd been a big baker from when she was little and stood on a stool to help her grand-mere on visits, but while she had a lot more use of her hand now, it didn't extend quite to pie crusts.

"You were home late last night. Was it a busy shift?" Lenka asked as she started to gather what she needed for the pumpkin pie.

"Not that late. I think it was about ten, but, yeah, it was busy. Lots of accidents and bubbling over family drama on Thanksgiving. Holidays are the happiest time of the year." Grace was clearly being sarcastic. She opened the oven to check on the bread cubes she was toasting for the stuffing.

Lenka wondered why it was still called stuffing when it wasn't stuffed in anything, but a lot of terms were strange like that. "It seems especially fraught with two big holidays so close together. What do you usually do for Christmas?"

"Work."

"You work both Thanksgiving and Christmas?" Grace had told her that she kept this Thanksgiving tradition every year. Lenka hadn't expected to hear that she also worked on Christmas. She didn't take very good care of herself. Lenka made a note to step up her helpfulness when she had full use of her arm.

"Yes. On Christmas Day, usually. My mom and I get together on Christmas Eve, so it works out."

"Are you and your mom close?" Lenka hadn't heard her talk about her mom and had rather assumed she was out of the picture.

"It's…complicated. She remarried a few years back, and I don't get along with her new husband. I still love my mom, but it makes everything a challenge. She spends Thanksgiving and Christmas Day with him and his kids. I get Christmas Eve." Grace shrugged.

Lenka might have been reading into the situation, but she was pretty sure that Grace was covering for some serious hurt with that shrug. At the same time, she'd built herself a close-knit friend community, judging by what Lenka had seen since she'd broken her arm. It made her happy to think that Grace had built that community. She wanted good things for her.

"Anyway," Grace said as she moved to the counter to chop onions. "Are you close with your parents?"

"Yes. I mean, regular close, I think. They're interested in me and supportive, but they're not friends like some people are with their parents. I am really close with my grand-mere. I spent school breaks with her growing up because my parents both worked. She lives in an area of her small town without a lot of children, or at least, not at the time. I think it's turning over some now. But that's neither here nor there. That's a funny expression, isn't it? Anyway, yeah, no kids then. So she spent lots of time being my playmate. It's why my French is so good and where I learned to bake. Even after I was old enough that I could have stayed home alone, I still went to stay with her because she was basically my best friend. Pathetic, right?" Even as she self-deprecated, she hoped Grace wouldn't think she was pathetic. It mattered what she thought.

"Not at all. I think it's sweet. I was really close with my grandma, too. She's responsible for me having this house." Grace waved the knife she'd been chopping with.

"Was it her house?" Lenka wondered why Grace needed a roommate if she'd inherited the house. Maybe she didn't like living alone. Although, the way she'd reacted to Lenka's arrival made that seem unlikely.

"No. Her house got sold so the equity could be split. Each of us grandkids got a lump of money for a down payment if we didn't already own houses. I got mine when I turned twenty-five, so I just moved in a couple of months before your arrival."

That explained a lot. Like why the place was so sparsely furnished. "And your cousins? Do they live around here, too?"

"Not anymore. Well, a couple live out in the suburbs, but they're on different paths in life, and we're not close. Others moved away for college and never moved back. Some grew up away."

"Whoa. How many cousins do you have?"

"That probably made it sound like more than it really is. There are six of us. I was the closest to Grandma. We lived nearby, and my mom worked, so I spent a lot of time at her house after school and stuff. I guess we're both grandma's girls."

Lenka liked that. "That's certainly how I identify, although I'd never thought of the term." Lenka was so grateful for her grand-mere. Hearing Grace talk about hers in the past tense made her even more grateful that hers was still alive and thriving in France.

They worked quietly for a few minutes, then Grace said, "Did you never have close friends at school? I mean, because you spent school breaks with your grand-mere because she was your best friend."

"Oh, I did have some friends, I suppose, but I always felt like something of an outsider. I got teased by some kids because I was out from a young age."

"Really?" Grace asked, a tone of amusement. "How young?"

Lenka laughed but waited to answer while she ran the blender to mix the pumpkin, tofu, sugar, and spices. When it was done, she said, "I had my first crush when I was seven. I followed that poor girl around like a puppy."

"Precocious. I didn't really know until college. I did have dates for things like homecoming and prom but never cared to keep dating, even though those things were often springboards into relationships for other people. I figured it was because high school boys were immature. I thought I'd find someone in college. I did, but it wasn't a boy." Grace threw a cheeky grin at her.

They talked about exes and crushes for a while, then the conversation turned naturally to other things. They never seemed to run out of things to talk about. It was lovely. Lenka felt time slip away when she was with Grace. It was easy to talk to her, easy to look at her.

Lenka felt a pang of discomfort when that thought occurred to her. She was supposed to be thinking those sorts of thoughts about Mackenzie. Obviously, Mackenzie was good-looking. Hot, even. But lately, their conversations weren't anything like the ones she was having with Grace. They were either cut short by one or the other of them having to run, or they just kind of petered out. They'd managed a little phone sex only once since Lenka had broken her arm. Granted, the cast wasn't exactly sexy, but before Lenka came to Portland, it had been one of their mainstays of connection.

She shook it off. They'd be fine once they were together again. When Mackenzie came to visit in less than a month, they'd explore Portland together when they weren't spending long hours holed up in their hotel room. It'd be just like when they'd traveled together after they'd first met.

Grace had kindly offered to let Mackenzie stay with them and lie to Overseas Stays about it, but Lenka felt uncomfortable about having wanton sex with Grace in the next room. She'd feel that way about anyone in the next room, but the fact that it would be Grace was particularly uncomfortable for reasons she didn't want to identify.

"Something on your mind?" Grace asked. "You've gone quiet over there."

They were on the final stretch of cooking now. Lenka was assembling a salad, and Grace was removing a green bean casserole from the oven.

"I was just thinking about Mackenzie's visit next month."

Grace smiled broadly. "I bet you can't wait."

"Yeah. That's just what I was thinking." The doorbell rang, which meant it was likely one of Lenka's friends. Grace's friends all knew to walk in. "I'll get it."

Lenka rubbed her belly and groaned. "I'm so full."

Grace echoed a groan back at her from her spot on the other end of the couch. "I know, right? I didn't need that third piece of pie." She paused to consider. "I wanted it, but I didn't need it."

Lenka chuckled. "Exactly, except for me, I think it was the slice of apple cake that Aubrey and Carissa brought that did me in. I didn't know that cake on Thanksgiving was a thing."

"It's not, but Aubrey isn't a pie person."

Lenka gasped. "That's it. I can't trust her as my doctor anymore."

Grace laughed. "It is a failing on her part, to be sure."

"It was a good day, though." She meant it. It had been so much fun. They'd eaten, some people had helped with cleanup while others had gone for a walk. There had been charades. Lenka couldn't believe people did that in real life, not just in books and movies, but it had been lots of fun. There had been rounds of dessert. Their friends had mixed well. At the end, as usually seemed to happen, someone had said they were heading out, and it had started a trend. The house went from full to just the two of them in a matter of about fifteen minutes of coats, pressing leftovers on people, and good-byes.

"It was. What do you think? Traditional Thanksgiving or day after Friendsgiving?"

"Absolutely Friendsgiving for me. Although, I appreciate Sue's family including me yesterday. But today was…really great." In large part, it had been great because Grace was there. She was really starting to feel like an important person in Lenka's life. A friend she wanted there for the big stuff. She improved things with her very presence.

"Well, then, when you're a big hotshot translator for the UN living in New York next year, you'll have to come back for Friendsgiving. You can bring Mackenzie. It'll be great."

That was her dream: living in New York with Mackenzie or near Mackenzie, at least, and translating at the UN. But it felt like she almost had to remind herself of that. Right now, she was more excited about the possibility of having a Friendsgiving with Grace again next year. But that was just because today had been great. New York was still her dream.

Right? She decided she didn't want to consider that too closely right then. Of course it was her dream. Just because she'd been having fun with Grace didn't mean she was losing sight of her long-term goal. "Calling UN translators hotshots is a drastic misunderstanding of the background role of UN translators."

"Still. It's a big deal, and you're well on your way. It's impressive. And Carissa was singing your praises at the hospital.

You're not overdoing it, are you? She said you're practically always on call, but you have classes and stuff."

"She's exaggerating. I don't get called that often, and I never take a call during class. Don't worry, Mom. I'm putting school first." Lenka regretted the mom joke as soon as she said it. It was weird, even as a joke. That was not at all how she thought of Grace.

Grace must have agreed because she pulled a face and chucked a pillow at Lenka, who caught it easily and held it on her lap before deciding that was too much pressure on her very full stomach. She propped it behind her back and slouched even more.

"How about a movie while we digest?"

"If you think it'll help."

"I don't know if it'll help, to be honest, but it's about all I'm up for. And tradition says that after everyone goes home on Friendsgiving, it's time for the first Christmas movie of the year."

"You're into Christmas movies?"

"I'm into ridiculing Christmas movies," Grace corrected. "Christmas romances, particularly."

"Oh well, let the games begin." Lenka settled even more firmly in the couch. She was happy to have spent the afternoon with friends and happy it was down to her and Grace.

CHAPTER FIFTEEN

Lenka was on her way to the ER. This time, she was happy about it. She liked getting called in for translating in any department, but when it was the ER, she always had an extra pep in her step thinking about how she might see Grace. The other reason she was excited was because the language needed was French. That was unusual because a lot of French speakers spoke English, especially ones who traveled to the US.

She was nearly there when she remembered it was Grace's day off, and her happiness balloon punctured a little. She used her badge, which always felt very official, to open the door to the ER and saw Maci sitting at the nurse's station. She walked over, smile on her face. Seeing Maci wasn't as fun as seeing Grace but still fun. "Hello."

"Oh hey," Maci said returning the smile. "I was hoping it would be you. I've got a gentleman in bay three who is having trouble telling us what's going on."

"That's what I'm here for. Lead the way."

Maci knocked on the wall and opened the curtain to reveal an older man lying in bed clutching his stomach and looking despondent. Lenka greeted him, and he perked up. "You speak French? Oh, thank goodness. I feel like all my English has left me."

Lenka patted his shoulder. "That can happen in times of stress. What's going on?"

She translated between him and Maci, then between him and his doctor, then between him and a tech who came to draw blood for labs, and then between him and his doctor again and Maci once more. They finally left him resting more comfortably while waiting for a bed to open upstairs and walked back to the nurse's station together.

"Thanks for that. It's amazing what a difference communication makes."

Lenka was on a bit of a high from having helped. "Right? It's why I love translating."

"You're really good at it. The way you were able to make a connection with the patient?" Maci made a chef's kiss motion. "You should make a career of it or something."

"You don't say." Lenka grinned at her. "I hope I can make a difference on an even wider scale at the UN."

Maci leaned against the nurse's station and looked doubtful.

"What?"

"I know there are all kinds of important things to do in the world, but don't dismiss the impact you just had on that gentleman."

Lenka was horrified. She hadn't meant to imply that the work Maci and Grace did wasn't important. Her functioning arm was proof of that. "I didn't mean it like that. I mean, of course it's important. I've just always wanted to work for the UN."

Maci gave her an easy smile. "Sure. I get it. And New York happens to be where your girlfriend lives, which sweetens the deal, no?"

"No. I mean yes." Yes was the answer, so why had she said no? She felt like the answer was just out of her grasp. It was true that her connection with Mackenzie wasn't as close these days. They were just going through a rough patch.

One of the other nurses called Maci. "Duty calls." She squeezed Lenka's arm and went to do her job.

Lenka leaned against the desk, thinking. She did still want New York and the UN and Mackenzie, right? Before she could get too deep into it, she saw Grace. Her spirits lifted at the sight. Somehow, Grace made the hospital scrubs look good. "What are you doing here? Isn't it your day off?"

"I got called in to cover for someone who's kid had some sort of emergency. I assume you're here showing off your linguistic abilities?" Grace smiled a smile that in combination with her words made Lenka feel seen.

"You know it. I'm all about showing off." She wrinkled her nose.

Grace laughed. "You do it without trying because you're that good."

Lenka waved her off, but she also felt warm from the praise.

"Oh, speaking of which, you said you know some Spanish, right? There's a patient in four who is a Spanish speaker. I was going to wait for Maria, but she's busy. Would you mind coming to talk to her with me?"

Lenka buzzed with the pleasure of being asked and needed. It was a different sort of buzz than she got with a usual request, but she wasn't sure why. Maybe because Spanish was a stretch language for her. "Of course not. My medical Spanish is still a work in progress, but let's see what we can do."

When Grace quickly squeezed her arm in thanks before leading the way, that felt like a reward in advance of the work.

❖

"It seems like you and Lenka are getting pretty close," Maci said.

They were sitting at the nurse's station together. Maci was waiting on a doctor for one of her patients and some tests for another. Grace had just sent someone home with a couple of Steri-Strips, and another of hers was off getting imaging done. She would get a new patient any minute but had a moment to breathe just then. Maci's mention of Lenka had her looking at the doors to the ED. It wasn't often that Lenka came through them, but it happened occasionally. It wasn't enough to justify how often she looked.

"We're friends for sure. I'll miss her after she leaves." They'd lately been in belly laughs over making fun of the Christmas movies together. It was more than that, but even losing that would be sad.

Maci was looking at her like she was being stupid.

"What?" Grace had a niggling sensation she knew what Maci was getting at. She regretted asking and turned to the computer ostensibly to ensure her charting was all in order.

"Grace Lillian Talcott. You have a crush on your host daughter."

Grace groaned. "That is gross in so many ways, Maci Catriona O'Sullivan." Two could play at the full name game. "Why would you say that, and why would you call her 'host daughter' while saying it? What is wrong with you?"

Maci held her hands up. "Fair enough. Now that you have a crush on her, I'll let that host daughter thing go."

"For crying out loud, Lenka has a girlfriend. A girlfriend who is coming to visit in a few weeks and for whom she's moving to New York. Also, dating your exchange student is verboten. Also, also, she's leaving in June."

"The lady doth protest too much."

Grace buried her face in her hands. She knew it was a bad habit she shouldn't do at work, but she just found herself doing it in stressful moments. She rationalized that it was okay because of all the hand washing and sanitizer she used. "I can't have a crush on her." She straightened. She was talking herself out of it as much as Maci. "And I don't. I'm allowed to be friends with women. Look at you. A woman. And a friend. But maybe not if you keep this up." The computer pinged with a notification. Grace pointed at it. "Looks like your patient's lab results are in. Get back to work, and let me live."

Maci scooted over just as there was another ping. "And you've got a new patient. Oh…a puker. Lucky you."

Grace groaned again. As she walked to the lobby to collect her patient, she mused over what Maci had suggested. Not suggested. Outright said. That Grace had a crush on Lenka. She wasn't wrong. Grace had known it on some level. The crush had probably started the first moment she'd laid eyes on her at the airport. She was just so freaking cute. It had grown after watching her translate for the patient in need with her freshly donned cast. It had settled down and made itself comfortable once they'd begun to spend time together at home during Lenka's recovery and Grace's unsolicited time off. Cohosting Friendsgiving hadn't exactly made it go away. And their new habit of ridiculing Christmas movies together meant the crush had started furnishing its new home.

She couldn't stop looking for Lenka at work. She couldn't stop her voice from piping up in her head when someone used an idiom that used to be commonplace but now was noteworthy. She couldn't stop thinking about the way she ran her finger up and down the length of her nose when she was thinking especially hard, which happened often when she was doing homework at the table. Every scent of vanilla had her pining. It was a mess.

"Patrick Farley?" Grace called into the waiting room.

A pale man clutching an emesis bag likely provided by the receptionist stood and came her way.

"Hi, there. Come this way." She led him back down the hall to an empty room while she continued to think over the problem. She wasn't unfamiliar with crushing on someone who didn't reciprocate. She'd pined for women before. Who hadn't? One of those crushes had been very strong. There'd been a nurse in charge of her rotation in surgery who had a whole stern, older woman thing going for her. She'd also been very good at her job, and competence was one of Grace's turn-ons. It was one of the reasons she was so drawn to Lenka. All those languages. But between being a combination of teacher and boss and the age gap, there'd never been a chance that her crush would develop into anything. After a while, it had faded away.

This one would, too. It just needed time. Likely meeting Mackenzie at Christmas would help. The presence of a girlfriend would have to be a turnoff, right?

The sound of retching pulled her back to the present moment. Luckily, the patient was using the bag. She patted his back and took the bag when he finished, depositing it in the proper waste receptacle as they passed.

"Here we go. You can get up on the bed or sit in the chair, whichever is more comfortable." Grace retrieved another bag out of one of the drawers and handed it to him. She pulled one of the wheeled computer stations into the room and asked, "How long has this been going on?"

When she was done with his exam and waiting on a doctor to check him, she discovered her patient who'd gone to imaging was back. Between one thing and another, she was kept busy for the rest of her shift. Her next chance to talk to Maci was when they were both changing after shift change.

"You're not wrong," Grace said.

"Of course not." Maci pulled her sweater over her head. "About what?"

Grace waved her hand. "The crush on Lenka."

"Oh, that. Of course I'm right. What are you going to do about it now that you've accepted reality?"

Grace pulled her boots on. "Nothing. It'll pass."

Maci looked at her skeptically.

"Really. Besides, she has a girlfriend. I can't make a move. What kind of person would I be if I did?"

"Maybe you're right." Maci pulled her tote bag out of her locker and slammed it shut. "Or maybe Lenka feels the same way."

Grace pulled her backpack onto one shoulder. "If so, then she needs to break it off with her girlfriend first. But I doubt she does. She's moving to New York to be with her."

"And to be a UN translator. I don't know, Grace." Maci held the door open for them both. "I think the translator part means more to her than the Mackenzie part. At least, that's the impression I've gotten when I've talked to her."

"Regardless, that means living in New York. It's doomed either way. I have no interest in a long-distance relationship or getting involved in something I know could only be temporary." Injecting her voice with all the resolution she could muster, she said, "It'll pass."

Chapter Sixteen

It was Friday morning, so Lenka didn't have any classes. She wasn't due at the hospital until afternoon, and Grace was at work. Mackenzie wasn't waiting tables and had hours until call time. They were finally going to be able to have a good long talk.

Lenka sent a message saying she was ready when Mackenzie was, settled back against her pillows, took a sip of coffee, and sighed in pleasure at the taste and warmth. This was going to be a good morning. Probably. The various times their calls had been cut short had left her feeling nowhere near as excited for them as she'd been a few months ago.

Her laptop chimed merrily with the incoming video call. "Hello."

Mackenzie smiled at her from the screen. "Hey, baby. Not long now until I see you in person."

Lenka mustered a smile in return. "I can't wait."

"How's your day been?"

"It's kind of just started. I've only been awake about an hour. But pretty good. Yours?"

"Same."

Lenka cast about for something to say. "How'd the show go last night?"

Mackenzie shrugged one shoulder. "It was fine. You know, the usual."

Lenka tried to think of a question that would start a longer conversation. *It shouldn't be this difficult, should it?* She thought about dinner with Grace the night before. They'd practically talked over each other in their excitement to share their days. The conversation had continued while they did the dishes, transitioning into talking about a book they'd both read. Mackenzie wasn't a reader, but maybe Lenka could get something going by bringing up one of the silly Christmas movies she and Grace had watched.

"Have you ever—"

But at the same time, Mackenzie started talking, "I was out with—"

Lenka stopped. She'd just been trying to get the conversation started. If Mackenzie had something to say, then she was all ears. "You go."

After a beat, Mackenzie began again with, "I was out with Piper after the show the other night and guess who we ran into?"

Lenka had no idea. It seemed a stretch to think it would be someone she knew. She'd never met any of Mackenzie's friends, but she had heard some names. "Rachel?"

Mackenzie laughed. "No. Darla."

"Oh." Lenka was pretty sure she'd never heard that name before.

"So, yeah. Anyway, what have you been up to?"

"School and volunteering at the hospital, mostly. But I—"

"All work and no play makes Lenka a dull girl. I'll have to come help you loosen up."

The interruption and sentiment made Lenka lose all desire to tell her about the stupid Christmas movie thing she and Grace had been doing. Instead, she tapped into the part of her that was excited. "Yes, that'll be good."

"Good? Okay." Mackenzie looked nonplused.

That was a strange word, nonplused. If it was meant like it was said, they were negatived. Which sort of made sense, but why not just say negatived? If it were more as it was spelled, then it would mean "no pulse." If someone didn't have a pulse, they'd be dead. Mackenzie didn't look dead, just unexcited. Long distance was tough.

They were quiet for a few moments, then Mackenzie picked up her phone. "Well, maybe I should get going. I'll see you soon, baby. Bye."

"Bye." But Lenka was pretty sure Mackenzie had clicked disconnect before she said it.

❖

"You seem really tired. Are you sure you're up for the movie?" Lenka peered at Grace across the table as she started gathering the empty dishes from dinner.

Grace stifled a yawn and straightened. She'd been looking forward to this for the last two days. She and Lenka had been missing each other due to work and school obligations, and even though she was very tired after a stretch of long days of work, she really wanted to watch a movie. It sounded better than sleep. "I'm fine."

Lenka shot her a skeptical look as she stood. "Okay, but you go get it ready and relax while I take care of the dishes. You've been working really hard."

It made Grace think of all those days of overtime she'd worked when Lenka had first arrived. At least then, she'd come home and gone right to bed. Now she was probably getting less sleep on long stretches thanks to having a standing evening plan.

Lenka looked over her shoulder. "What are you smiling about?"

"Nothing. Just how things have changed since you first got here."

"You mean how you stopped ignoring me? All it took was me breaking my arm. The extreme measures I had to go to." Lenka laughed.

Grace chuckled in return but also winced. She still felt guilty about Loki. "I do like to play hard to get." Oops. She hadn't meant that to sound like flirting.

Lenka just laughed again.

It was only a few minutes before they were settled on the couch with the opening strains of Christmas music. And just a few minutes more until the credits were rolling. Or at least, so it seemed to Grace.

She was on her side, head pillowed on something warm. Hadn't she been sitting up? Oh shit. Her head was on Lenka's lap.

Did Lenka know? How could she not? Maybe she'd fallen asleep, too? She must have because wasn't that Lenka's hand on her shoulder?

Grace shifted toward sitting, and Lenka's hand immediately lifted. "I'm sorry. I seem to have fallen asleep on you." Grace was beyond embarrassed. She'd been trying very hard not to let her feelings for Lenka show. They were inappropriate at best, and here she'd fallen asleep on her. She couldn't look at her.

Lenka stretched and shifted away. "It's not a problem," she said through a yawn.

At that, Grace did sneak a peek. Was she blushing? No. Her cheeks must have flushed from sleep. "Well," Grace said, "I think this is a sign we should both go to bed. Our own beds, I mean." Why had she said that? She wanted to bury her face in her hands. Instead, she quickly stood and started to walk away, only to find herself tangled in the blanket. Oh God, could this get any more awkward?

Lenka steadied her with a hand on her elbow. "Are you okay?"

"Fine, fine. Sleep muddled, I think," she mumbled as she bent to pick up the blanket and toss it over the back of the couch. She fled before she could embarrass herself any more.

When she came out after sleeping in the next morning, the whole thing seemed like a dream. A good dream or a nightmare, she couldn't quite decide. The blanket was neatly folded on the back of the couch, and Lenka was in the kitchen sipping coffee. She greeted Grace normally. Maybe she really had dreamed the whole thing.

Chapter Seventeen

Lenka was forty-five minutes into the hour-long public transportation journey taking her to the airport. It was finally the day of Mackenzie's arrival.

This journey was ridiculous. Grace's house was actually quite close to the airport, but the only way to get there via public transit was to first ride a bus south, then transfer to the MAX to go east, and then back north. Aside from maybe New York, Portland had one of the better public transportation systems in the US, or so Lenka had been told. And yet, here she was.

She was planning on springing for an Uber to get to the hotel. After some internal debate about where to stay, she had chosen a hotel in the Lloyd district that was directly on the MAX line and would be a good base for doing touristy things. She wanted everything to be as nice as possible for Mackenzie. She was flying all the way across the country to visit, after all.

The other hotel option Lenka had seriously considered was the Kennedy School, which had a lot of local flavor and was in Grace's neighborhood. While it would have been nice for showing Mackenzie around her stomping grounds, it was less accessible for nearly everything else. And for some reason, she wasn't excited about Grace and Mackenzie meeting. The farther away they stayed, the less likely they'd run into each other unexpectedly.

Lenka checked her phone. Another ten minutes until she got to the airport. Because she'd wanted to make sure she was on time, she'd left plenty early. So even after she got there, she'd be waiting for another half an hour or so.

She was excited. And nervous. The nerves had surprised her with their presence a couple of days prior and had only grown from there. Lately, it felt like she and Mackenzie were not in sync. They had a hard time finding time for calls, and when they did talk, they didn't seem to have much to talk about. But she should have also been excited. She and Mackenzie had chemistry in person. This visit couldn't be happening at a better time, she told herself firmly. She'd reconnect with Mackenzie and reconnect with the excitement she used to have about moving to New York.

It wasn't that she didn't want to translate for the UN anymore. She did. Certainly. But being in Portland had expanded her horizons in lots of ways. She really liked the city and was sad at the idea of leaving at the end of the school year. She ran her hand through her newly green hair. If she worked for the UN, would she have to have a natural hair color? She fit in here.

If stereotypes were to be believed, the people in New York were not friendly, whereas most people in Portland had been friendly and welcoming, from Willa at the coffee shop to all of Grace's friends.

She also liked translating at the hospital. It was so rewarding. And it allowed her to stretch herself in different ways from the simultaneous translating she was trying to perfect for her certification. At the hospital, she got to use a bunch of different languages. If she got the UN job, she'd use two or three at most.

But translating at the UN would mean helping with concepts as large as world peace. Potentially.

That was the problem right there. The work at the UN was big and important, but Maci had a point. Helping one person at a time was real. The UN had a lot of lofty ideals but no real power. Meanwhile, translating at the hospital meant immediate impact. Lenka felt pulled toward that tangible result. Of course, she could find a job translating at a hospital in New York. But was living in New York still her dream?

Maybe. The answer was maybe.

She jiggled her knee up and down with nerves. She should know this. She should know if she was excited or dreading Mackenzie's visit. Man, was she ever a bad girlfriend.

The train pulled into the airport stop, accompanied by the announcement that it was the end of the line, and all passengers had to disembark. Lenka shook herself. Mackenzie had come all this way to see her. It wasn't the time to be questioning if she was still in on their plans. She was. She had to be. Otherwise, what was all this for?

She went inside and checked the boards that told her the same thing the flight tracker on her phone had said; Mackenzie's flight was due to land ten minutes early. Due to her overly cautious cushion, Lenka still had another twenty minutes to wait. She considered calling Grand-mere for a boost of moral support, but it was likely past her bedtime. Plus, Grand-mere had met Mackenzie when Lenka had brought her along during their travels and had been a little reserved about her. It had surprised Lenka because Mackenzie was very fun-loving, and so was Grand-mere.

When Lenka had asked Grand-mere about it, she'd just smiled and said that if Mackenzie made her happy, that was all she needed to hear. Lenka had assured her that was the case, but she'd gotten the feeling that if she'd expressed any doubt, Grand-mere would have encouraged that doubt rather than feed any sort of excitement about reuniting.

Lenka paced the length of the airport alongside the food court and the shops. Her mind drifted back to excitement versus anxiety. She was worried that the chemistry wouldn't be there and worse, that they weren't a good long-term fit. Lenka liked evenings on the couch, particularly evenings with Grace recently, while Mackenzie was out till all hours after evening performances. Yes, they both enjoyed travel, and yes, the idea of living in New York had bonded them with Mackenzie already there and it being one of Lenka's potential dreams.

Only potential. When they'd met, Lenka had already been dreaming of translating for the UN, but she'd have been as happy in New York as at the Hague. She'd shifted her entire dream to New

York solely because that was where Mackenzie lived. But if she and Mackenzie weren't a good fit anymore, then what was Lenka's dream?

Ugh. She needed to stop this. She had to switch to excitement. Mackenzie was coming to see her at no small cost. It was going to be good. She stopped in a store and bought a stuffed animal and some chocolates to welcome Mackenzie to Portland. She was already blowing her budget big-time by paying for the hotel, why not overextend a little more? She needed something to shift into excitement.

She took her gifts and stood under the arrival information boards where passengers came out of security. Mackenzie's flight had landed. She could be coming out those doors any minute.

Lenka's mind flashed back to seeing Grace standing in nearly this very spot, holding that glittery sign. Grace had looked so tired and so surprised. Lenka should have known that a wire had been crossed somewhere, but she'd been too tired and jet-lagged herself to put the pieces together. Still, even with all that, Grace had been such a sight for sore eyes. Of course, she'd represented the end of Lenka's journey, but it had been more than that. Lenka had noticed her before the sign, sparkly as it was. Grace had been all curves in her jeans and T-shirt. Her bangs had framed a face that was best described as kind. Her eyes, even makeup-less as they'd been that night, seemed smoky. Lenka had found her attractive. But noticing someone's attractiveness wasn't the same as being attracted to them.

No, that had come later. Lenka bit her lip. It felt traitorous, but it was true. She was attracted to Grace. Watching her cook for her friends and effortlessly entertain, seeing her day in and day out in all sorts of different clothes and all sorts of different moods, the way she'd cared for Lenka at the hospital and then in little ways while she'd been in her cast, all of that was what attracted Lenka to her.

She felt like banging her head on the wall. She should have recognized all this the evening that Grace had fallen asleep on her lap. She'd been so tired, she'd drifted off before the movie had even really started. Lenka had told herself she hadn't wanted to disturb her when she'd eased her down and settled her head on her lap. But really, she'd wanted the contact. She'd let the whole movie play, but she'd spent most of it looking at Grace sleeping peacefully. She'd even put her hand on her, practically cuddling her. On purpose. She'd been so embarrassed when Grace had woken up. How was she supposed to explain their position? But when Grace had seemed to assume they'd both been asleep, she'd let it ride.

If she'd admitted her feelings to herself a couple of weeks ago, she could have called Mackenzie off. Now, she felt like she needed to give this a real try. And there she was. Mackenzie was coming toward her, arms extended, smile on. It was time to see what was still there or what could be rekindled. Lenka smiled back and pulled her into a hug.

The conversation was a little stilted as they rode in the Uber to the hotel. Lenka was reduced to filling the silence by playing tour guide. "The river you probably saw when you were landing is called the Columbia. It runs east to west. Then there's the Willamette that runs south to north. It goes straight through Portland. One of the things we'll do if the weather holds is walk along it."

After she said it, she second-guessed everything. It was dark already, so even if Mackenzie had a window seat, could she have seen the water? Well, sure, at least as a dark section between the lights on either side. How was this what she was thinking about when she'd just picked up the girlfriend she hadn't seen in months? Shouldn't she have been thinking about getting her to the hotel room and having her way with her?

Mackenzie gave Lenka a smoldering look. "That is, if I ever let you leave the hotel room."

There it was. That was what Lenka should have been thinking about, but instead, she felt uncomfortable. If she'd been on the receiving end of that look even a month ago—for sure two months ago—she'd have been feeling hot under the collar. Why was it collar? It didn't matter right now. What mattered was that she should have been wanting to rip Mackenzie's clothes off. Now, the idea seemed forced, and she felt nothing but awkward. Shit. This wasn't going to work. The reality of Mackenzie sitting beside her was enough to know that.

On the other hand, maybe if they spent a day or so just being together, it would click again. Either way, the least Lenka could do was show Mackenzie a good time in Portland, so she smiled. "Let me take you to dinner. We'll get settled in the hotel, and then I've got a place picked out for tonight."

"I am hungry. I got busy and didn't pack well for the plane. I didn't want to pay for the overpriced sandwiches, so I made do with the cookie they handed out and a packet of Saltines in my purse. Where are we going? Someplace Portland-y?"

Lenka smiled a real smile now, relieved to have sidestepped the sex talk. "Oma's Hideaway. It's kind of pan Asian, but mostly southeast Asian. We've got a lot of good Asian restaurants here. It's not super fancy, but I figured you might be tired. I have reservations for us for fancy tomorrow night."

The next night was Christmas Eve, and Lenka had thought something special was in order. Honestly, as fancy as it was going to be, she was still bummed to be missing Christmas Eve at Grace's. Grace would be having brunch with her mom, then going home to cook for friends. Lenka would have been happier hanging with the gang.

Wow, had she ever messed this up.

Grace had invited Lenka and Mackenzie, but Lenka had declined. She'd made the reservation months ago, thinking that she wanted the time alone with Mackenzie, and lately, she'd had that strange feeling that she didn't want Mackenzie and Grace to meet.

"We? Have you gone native? Nothing beats New York cuisine. We've got everything. You'll see."

New York did have everything. Or at least, that was its reputation. Maybe Lenka should at least visit before she made any life-altering decisions. Not that she felt in a position to make any decisions just then. She felt adrift. She knew she wanted to be a translator. Everything else seemed nebulous.

"I do really like it here. I think you'll love it, too."

"Yeah? Tell me what you like about it."

"Well..." Lenka no sooner thought of a reason than she discarded it. Everything seemed centered around Grace. Finally, she came up with something. "I like that I fit in here. Nearly everyone I meet is queer in some way, and every fourth person has a fun hair color. And tattoos, nearly everyone has tattoos."

"That's all true in New York, too. You'll like it there."

Lenka wanted to come up with a reason to prove otherwise, but all she could think of were inane things. "There are the food carts. We'll have to go to a pod. It's cool because everyone can get whatever they want and still eat together."

Mackenzie wrinkled her nose. "You want us to go sit outside in the rain to eat from a roach coach?"

"It's not like…" Lenka trailed off. She felt on the defensive and didn't want to feel that way. She didn't have to prove anything. She'd show Mackenzie around the city, and either they'd connect again or not. Either way, Lenka would have more information for planning her future. "We don't have to, but we'll see how things go. You're only here a few days, and lots of things are closed for Christmas anyway. Meanwhile, tonight, we've got Oma's Hideaway. Tell me about your flight. And what had you so busy?"

Mackenzie talked for the rest of the drive while Lenka made appropriate listening noises and fretted about her life choices.

Chapter Eighteen

While she cooked, Grace filled the house with Christmas music that heavily favored pop artists from the last decade. The house had felt empty since Lenka had left the day before to go meet Mackenzie at the airport. Grace had offered her a ride, but she'd said she was fine to go alone.

Grace tried not to feel slighted. It was reasonable that Lenka wanted time alone with her girlfriend, but she did wonder if she was going to get to meet her at all. They weren't even coming for dinner tonight. It was like real life had come to town to put Grace in her place in Lenka's life.

That was fine. It was a good reminder.

And life without Lenka was fine. She was looking forward to hanging out with her friends this evening. It was an open house situation going from four to eleven-ish to accommodate people who worked today and people who needed to get up early for day shift tomorrow. That included Grace, and she knew from experience that she'd be a little tired tomorrow, but what was one tired day compared to the joy of hosting a get-together for her friends?

Still, she wished Lenka was there. She had a hard time getting scenes of them in the kitchen out of her mind. They always had such a good time cooking together, even when it was just for the two of them. They often talked about their days, but sometimes, they sang along to whatever playlist one or the other put on. They had a similar taste in music, so it was often hard to tell who'd pressed play.

She flashed to last week when they'd gotten carried away singing along with Lady Gaga. Grace had held a wooden spoon up to her mouth and ended up with marinara on her chin. Lenka had laughed, then moved close to assist. For one brief, wild moment, Grace had thought Lenka's thumb would move up less than an inch and brush her lip.

She firmly stopped that line of thinking. Lenka was off-limits. This visit from Mackenzie was, indeed, a good reminder.

She refocused on the music. Loki continually jumping up on the counters to investigate the food was also a good distraction. What really made the difference was when Maci came bursting in with Greg on her heels.

"I'm here, the party can start."

"Merry Christmas," Greg called, holding up a bottle of wine in each hand.

"Merry Christmas, you guys." Grace wiped her hands on a dish towel and gathered them into a hug.

"Whoa. Feeling sentimental?" Maci asked.

"Maybe a little. Come keep me company while I finish up in the kitchen."

"Need any help? Because I will not hesitate to send Greg over there." Maci wasn't a cook. That was why she always brought wine. Greg was the one who did the little cooking at their place, but they relied heavily on takeout and convenience foods.

Grace playfully blocked the way to the stove. "No way. But you can certainly open up the wine." They worked on that while Grace plated a few more things and moved the Crock-Pots to the island for a self-serve buffet.

Maci handed her a glass of wine. "It's weird Lenka isn't here. I've gotten really used to her colorful self."

"You and me both, my friend."

Maci regarded her. "You doing okay?"

"Why wouldn't she be?" Greg asked as he dipped a chip.

"Because she has a big ol' crush on Lenka."

Greg looked at her wide-eyed. "You do?"

"Nah. I mean, it's a little crush."

"Big ol' crush," Maci reiterated. "How could you not have noticed?"

He shrugged. "I'm a dude."

Maci rolled her eyes. "Why was I cursed to be straight?"

Greg put his arm around her and kissed her temple. "It's your cross to bear, but I'm here for you in your time of crisis."

She giggled. "You're not so bad."

"Glad to hear it."

Grace watched them with a small smile. They were so cute. She was glad Maci had found her person. Lenka couldn't possibly be Grace's. It was just a little crush to get past.

Voices and a cool breeze of air announced the arrival of more guests. The party built quickly from there. This was Grace's big one each year. While she held lots of smaller dinner parties, something this big with this much cooking was a once a year deal. She invited everyone, which explained why several of Lenka's friends stopped by, even though she wasn't there. That included Carson, who'd been a fixture at their combined dinner parties, and Sue, who'd dropped by with her entire host family, all of whom thanked her profusely for inviting them. They didn't stay long because they had an evening get-together with family, but it was nice to see them, even though it reminded Grace Lenka wasn't there.

Tess and Maci had even managed to say a few polite words before they went their separate ways to talk to people they liked better. Tess was a good person, which was why Grace had said yes to that first date last spring. She just wasn't Grace's person. For one thing, she liked eating out where Grace liked gathering friends at home. Lenka likes hosting dinner parties, too, her treacherous mind reminded her.

Tess approached, helping to wrench Grace's mind away from Lenka once more. "Good get-together, Grace."

"Thanks, Tess. What're your plans for tomorrow?"

Tess pulled a face. "I'm working. It's fine, though, because I have New Year's Eve off, and that's the important one. I've got big plans for going to a club with friends and getting very drunk."

Grace smiled at that, glad it wasn't her plan. That was another reason they weren't good together. Grace liked wine, enough to get silly sometimes, but she hated loud clubs and getting so drunk that she wished she was dead the next morning. Lenka wasn't into partying, either. Yet another reason Grace liked her.

After much eating, drinking, and being merry, with plenty of comings and goings, it was nearly eleven. Grace started cleaning up as a gentle reminder to the guests that it was time to clear out. Maci, loyal to the end, was in the kitchen with her, loading the dishwasher. Greg was collecting orphaned plates and glasses from various spots. Carissa was helping load up storage containers with leftovers. Aubrey, who'd had a busy day at work before arriving, was helping by finishing off the last of a plate of food. The stragglers were popping into the kitchen to say good-bye and take their leave.

"Good shindig as always, Grace," Aubrey said from her perch on one of the barstools at the island.

The others echoed the sentiment.

"Thanks, guys. It's what makes Christmas for me, so I'm glad you enjoy it, too." It was nothing but the truth. Ever since her grandma had died and her mom had gotten married, the traditions of Friendsgiving and the Christmas Eve open house were the things that had kept her going through the holidays.

"It's totally what makes Christmas for me, too," Carissa said. "With my family in Indiana and Aubrey working over the holidays, it wouldn't feel like Christmas without a Grace party."

That sort of sentiment was music to her ears. It was her goal to create a space for her friends that felt like home. Still, a little of the shine was off because Lenka wasn't there. She knew she only had Lenka as a roommate for a short time, but while she was there, she was family, and it was sad that she'd missed the big party of the year. She'd have loved it, all these people to talk to.

Grace felt the draft of cold that meant the front door had opened and wondered who'd forgotten what. She stuck her head into the living room to see. "Lenka? What are you doing here? Did you forget something? Is Mackenzie with you?"

Lenka stood, arms akimbo, looking lost. "Mackenzie left. I came home because she left."

CHAPTER NINETEEN

Dinner at Oma's Hideaway was fine. The food was quite good. There weren't a lot of vegetarian options on the menu, but the dish Lenka had chosen was so good, she hadn't missed more. Mackenzie seemed to enjoy her dish as well, but she did make a point to compare it to her favorite Asian restaurant in New York that was even better, so she said.

What was only fine was the conversation. It was practically like first date talk. Getting to know you chitchat. But underlined by the discomfort that they were supposed to know each other well. All it did was highlight the fact that they barely talked these days. Lenka didn't know most of the names Mackenzie referenced. To be fair, Mackenzie's social group shifted every time she was in a new production, so it was difficult to keep up, but Lenka should have known the names of the people her girlfriend spent so much time with.

On the other hand, the only name Mackenzie seemed to recognize from Lenka's stories was Grace. But Lenka also talked about Sue and Carson quite often. She could see how Mackenzie might not know all her classmates, or even all of the exchange students she spent time with, but those two had been her best friends in Portland. Lenka wasn't sure if that meant that she hadn't told Mackenzie enough about her life or if it meant that Mackenzie hadn't been paying attention. Neither was great.

Lenka took care of the check and in an effort to put off going back to the hotel room, said, "Should we go for a drink before we head back?"

Mackenzie looked enthused. "Maybe at a club? Someplace we can dance?"

"Let's do it." Lenka had to look up clubs because it wasn't an activity she'd done since living in Portland. She wasn't big on loud crowds in general. She found one listed as LGBTQ+ friendly not too far away.

They had a good time dancing, but she was glad when they called it a night. The noise and press of bodies had gotten to the overwhelming stage. The best part was that when they finally made it to their hotel, Lenka emerged from her turn in the shower to find Mackenzie already passed out in bed. She slipped in next to her, careful not to wake her, and tried to sleep. Unfortunately, her mind had other ideas. Eventually, though, she fell into a fitful sleep.

She awoke to someone smoothing her hair. Probably Grace. She was very nurturing. She leaned into the touch. It was a nice way to wake up. Lenka opened her eyes to see Mackenzie nose to nose with her. She became fully awake, startled back, then attempted to relax.

"Hey, there," Mackenzie said. "Bad dream?"

"Must have been," Lenka said, not meaning it. "How'd you sleep?"

"I slept like a baby, but I'm sorry I fell asleep on you last night. Let me make it up to you." She got a come-hither look in her eye and leaned in. Lenka stiff-armed her. Mackenzie sat up, fire in her eyes. "What the fuck, Lenka? What's going on?"

Lenka felt horrible. She'd encouraged Mackenzie to come but now didn't want her here. To be fair, it wasn't until a day or two ago that she'd realized that. And she did want to show her a good time, regardless of if she still wanted her as a girlfriend. If she was honest, maybe they could still have a good time as friends. They'd had fun dancing the night before. She should have told Mackenzie last night instead of dodging.

She sat up, too, and pulled her knees to her chest. "I'm so sorry. I have had some realizations in the last couple days."

"That you aren't interested in me? After I flew all the way to this stupid city?"

Lenka wanted to protest on behalf of Portland, but that wasn't the important thing right now. "That I don't think we should be girlfriends. I don't know exactly when it happened, but at some point in the last couple of months, I think we can both agree, we drifted apart."

Mackenzie rolled her eyes. "Of course we have. But so what? We can still have fun. Besides, I never really considered us girlfriends."

"You…what?"

"Girlfriends. How can we be? We don't live in the same city or until recently, the same country. We're—I don't know—friends with benefits or something. It's not like we're exclusive. I just came out to visit you for a good time."

Revelations were hitting Lenka like little gut punches. "We're not…you haven't been…you see other people?"

Mackenzie laughed. "Of course I do. Have you really not been?"

"We did say we were girlfriends. It was a conversation. When we were traveling together. I was going to move to New York to be with you."

"We were travel girlfriends. We were exclusive then. I figured it was obvious that we'd each just"—she waved her hand—"do our thing. And when you came to New York, we'd date and see what happened from there. You were coming to New York for school and for the UN."

Lenka could see how they'd gotten their wires crossed. However, even though she didn't want to be with Mackenzie now, it still hurt. Their whole relationship had been amazingly one-sided, practically fantasy on Lenka's part. That hurt.

"Oh, baby." Mackenzie laid a sympathetic hand on Lenka's arm. "You really thought this was something else, didn't you?"

The was no point denying it. "I did. But here we are. What do you want to do now?"

"We could still fuck."

"I'm not feeling that."

Mackenzie shrugged. "Then, again, I'm wondering why I'm here."

"When we planned it, I thought you were coming to see your girlfriend, and of course, I thought we would be having sex. I didn't understand my own feelings about all that until very recently. And I had no idea you were just coming for a few days of sex with someone you once dated and might again. So, yeah, me too on the wondering why you're here thing."

Mackenzie huffed. "Listen, this could have been fun, but it's not worth it." She grabbed her phone off the nightstand. "I'm going to see if I can change my flight. I've got friends doing a thing tomorrow, and I'd rather be there than here."

Lenka felt stunned. She got out of bed and went to the bathroom to think in peace. As she brushed her teeth and washed her face, her brain cleared. She was feeling a lot of things, but she couldn't deny that one of the foremost things was relief. Mackenzie going home meant she could go home, too. Home to Grace. Her spirits lifted at the thought. And she clearly hadn't hurt Mackenzie by rejecting her, aside from thwarting her holiday plans. By the time she emerged, she was hopeful that Mackenzie had found a flight that was leaving right away.

"My new flight is at midnight, so we've got some time to kill. How about you take me to breakfast for my troubles?"

Lenka wasn't at all sure that she owed Mackenzie anything at this point, but she resigned herself to a day of sightseeing with her…ex? She wasn't sure how to classify her after their talk this morning. Did believing she was in a relationship mean she'd been in one? From the perspective of her emotions, yes. Or no. She still wasn't sure. Lately, her emotions had been more tied up with Grace. She didn't feel heartbroken, that was for sure, but not every breakup necessarily meant a broken heart. She was a little angry. She felt foolish.

But primarily, as she'd realized in the bathroom, she felt relieved.

"Fine. What are your thoughts on doughnuts?"

They ended up having a good day. They stood in a long line for Voodoo Doughnuts, walked on the Esplanade, saw the Christmas tree in Pioneer Courthouse Square, grabbed a bite at a food cart that Mackenzie admitted was pretty good, did some shopping, and showed up for their reservation for the fancy dinner.

Still, once Lenka dropped Mackenzie off at the airport, she felt relief to the point of near giddiness.

She could go home now. She didn't want to take the time it would take to take MAX and then the bus, but she was also feeling sensitive about all the money she'd spent in the past thirty hours. She chose to put in the time. Besides, it would give her the space to shift from tour guide back to herself. Because the person she was here in Portland did feel like her much more than she ever had felt like herself with Mackenzie.

She still wasn't sure what she wanted in the future. Provided she graduated…okay, she wasn't worried about graduation. She was worried about the translator's test that she would have to pass after. She was good, but the test was hard, and she wasn't necessarily United Nations good. They took the best of the best.

But was that even what she wanted?

She really didn't know.

What she did know was that it was Christmas Eve, and she was headed home. She was going to get to see Grace. When she got there, she waved to a couple of people who were leaving as she walked up. Others were still inside. The party wasn't entirely over. She recognized Maci's car parked out front.

She let herself in and heard voices and the sounds of dishes clanking, the sounds of a small group of people who were comfortable with one another. She took off her coat and stood to bask in it.

How could this feel so much like home? She didn't think she'd felt this way since she'd arrived at Grand-mere's for a long summer break the last time she'd gone. She had gone from so happy to be there to worried about losing this sense of home in a split second.

Grace stuck her head out of the passage to the kitchen and dining room. "Lenka? What are you doing here?"

She said something else, but Lenka snagged on that question. What was she doing there? She'd come home, but this wasn't really home. It was temporary. She felt bereft, as if mourning a loss that hadn't happened yet. She couldn't put any of that into words, so what she said was, "Mackenzie left. I came home because she left."

Then, Grace was hugging her, and everyone else came out of the kitchen to see what was happening. Grace explained, and they were all hugging her. These people were wonderful, but she was only here temporarily. This was home but not. Lenka burst into tears.

Chapter Twenty

Grace felt bad about going to work on Christmas. She didn't usually. It was no big deal for her. The day hadn't been special since her grandma had died. But today, it felt wrong to leave Lenka. She'd come home so sad last night. She had gone to bed shortly after. Grace had wanted to be there for her today, the Christmas she was spending away from family and now also from Mackenzie. She must really have loved Mackenzie to be so upset.

The day went by in the usual flurry of holiday mishaps. Most notable was a group of siblings who'd dared each other to stuff some of their new toys various places. But the category also included a carving knife to a foot and an accidental—probably—poisoning. She messaged Lenka a couple of times to check on her and got bland responses that worried her.

She got lucky and was able to leave on time, not always guaranteed on a holiday, for reasons ranging from frequent calling in sick to lots of patients. She was headed to the locker room to change when Aubrey found her. "How's Lenka? She seemed really worked up last night."

"I don't know, really. She's been rather evasive today. I don't know if…"

"If what?"

"If I've come on too strong." Maybe Lenka felt hounded by the check-in messages rather than cared for. Maybe she needed space to process.

"What do you mean? Did you make a move?" Aubrey seemed more excited than alarmed about the possibility.

"No. Of course not. She had a girlfriend up until yesterday. And there are policies against dating your exchange student."

"Come on. Does that really apply here? She's older than you."

"Yeah, but there is still a power imbalance. I'm in charge of her housing and food and everything."

Aubrey looked thoughtful. "Huh. I guess that's true. I just wonder—"

"Aubrey, there you are," Michelle, one of the night shift nurses called from just down the hall. "We need you."

"Looks like I'm not getting out of here yet," Aubrey said. "Get out while you can. Run for your life." The last was said as she walked backward.

Grace chuckled. Poor Aubrey. She must have been as tired as Grace. She'd worked yesterday, then had shut the party down last night in addition to working today. Grace at least had gotten to sleep in yesterday, and the only taxing thing she'd done before beginning to prepare for the party was brunch with her mom.

She considered her mom while she changed. There was no circumstance under which an outside observer would consider their relationship a good one. They only saw each other a few times a year. Christmas Eve and Grace's birthday were guaranteed, but there was usually one more lunch in there somewhere. They were polite, catching up on one other's lives. But that wasn't a mother-daughter relationship. That was as close to estranged as they could be without being estranged.

Her mom had become a mother before she'd been ready for it. She was only twenty when Grace was born, and as Grace understood it, only went through with the pregnancy because her mother, Grace's grandma, had promised to help. And she had. It had been to Grandma's house that Grace went after school. She'd spent plenty of weekends there, too. She'd slept at home about the same amount of time she'd slept at Grandma's. Sometimes, Grace had wondered why she didn't just live with Grandma. When her mom had started dating her now husband when Grace was a teenager, she practically had moved in with Grandma. Her mom had gotten busy with Rich and his two kids. They'd gotten married after Grace went to college, and that was when she'd started only seeing her mom a few times a year.

Grace sometimes wondered why she bothered. She liked tradition. And it was her closest tie to her grandma, but she suspected it was more duty than enjoyment for both of them. Every time they saw each other, her mom inquired about her dating life. To give her some credit, she hadn't batted an eye about the fact that Grace was gay, but Grace wasn't sure if that was because she was really cool with it or if she simply didn't care enough about Grace to care whom she dated.

Yesterday, Grace had said, "No, not dating anyone."

"It's been a while."

That had stuck with her. It had been a while. She'd gone on a couple of dates with Tess less than a year ago, but that hadn't been worth telling her mother about. And before that? It had been college. So, yeah, a while. But Grace wasn't into dating just to date. She wanted a real connection, someone she could see a future with. If she wanted to spend time with people just for fun, well, that was what friends were for. And she had plenty of friends. She wasn't lonely.

But she also did have a desire for the closeness of a relationship. For someone who was her person. Maci was sort of her person, but she was also Greg's.

It had all boiled down to making her think that she should get out there and date. She wouldn't keep dating anyone she didn't click with, but if she didn't try, how would she meet someone?

Her heart jumped in and told her that she had met someone. Why didn't she just date Lenka? She told her treacherous heart to be quiet. Lenka was off-limits. And even if she wanted to skirt the rules about dating her exchange student and Lenka was on board, which was quite the leap to take, Lenka was still leaving in June. If Grace was looking for her person, she needed to look for someone who didn't have plans to live on the other side of the continent.

As she drove home, she decided it was time to put herself out there. It would distract her from looking for love in a place simply too close to home.

When she parked in front of her house, she wasn't sure what to expect. Would the house be dark, with Lenka in her room heartbroken? Would she be drunk and listening to loud music? Having an ice cream and rom-com party? The lights were on, so Grace was expecting one of the latter options; what she hadn't expected were the enticing smells that welcomed her the moment she opened the door.

Her home was warm, bright, and seasoned by the smells of sweet and savory mixing together. She stood for a moment, dumbfounded, before stripping off her coat and kicking off her boots. She let her nose lead her to the kitchen. Before she made it, Lenka popped her head out.

"Hey, I thought you'd come in. Merry Christmas." She seemed fine. Better than fine. She seemed upbeat. And she'd clearly been cooking and baking, judging by the smell. People stress baked, of course, but that didn't seem to be happening here. Either Lenka was putting on a very good face, or she was actually fine. It was likely the latter because nothing about her warm smile seemed fragile.

"Merry Christmas. It smells like you've been busy."

Lenka's smile grew. "I made some Czech favorites. Adjusted to be vegan, of course. Sometimes, those adjustments made them less Czech than would be recognized by a Czech person." She shrugged. "But I think it all turned out."

"It sure smells like it."

"Do you need a minute, or do you want to come eat?"

Grace did need a minute. She needed to adjust to the new circumstance of a happy, welcoming Lenka. "Just let me go clean up."

"And put on your soft clothes. This is meant to be a fun but no pressure, welcome home, small Christmas thing. I know you come home from work tired. So eat, and then you can go to bed or whatever."

"I…okay. Thanks. Be right back."

As Grace took a quick shower to wash the ED off and slipped into her joggers and a soft hoodie, she marveled at Lenka's quick recovery. She'd seemed so upset the night before, and now she was just fine? It was strange. But everyone reacted to separation in different ways. Perhaps her relationship with Mackenzie wasn't as serious as it had seemed from the outside. At any rate, this was a further sign that Grace should stay far away from any involvement with her. Lenka would never take it seriously.

As a friend, though, Lenka was gold. When Grace finally made it to the kitchen, there were places set at the table and a feast spread in front of her.

"This is amazing. It all looks and smells fabulous. Tell me about it all."

"Okay, well, this is something approaching bílá fazolová polévka with what we had on hand. It's...close enough."

It looked to be a creamy vegetable and bean soup and smelled delicious. Grace's stomach grumbled. It had been a busy day, and she'd only gotten a short break for lunch. The two cookies she'd practically inhaled from the plate that someone had brought in for Christmas around midday were not holding up well.

Lenka laughed. "Let's start with that." She ladled them each some soup.

Grace dug in. She was a few spoonfuls in before she was able to slow down enough to say, "This is so good."

Lenka beamed.

Grace melted. The soup, more food to come, the long day, and Lenka's smile all combined to make her practically turn into goo. Shit. She wasn't supposed to do that. Lenka was off-limits. She straightened, reminded herself that they were friends, and applied herself to her soup.

CHAPTER TWENTY-ONE

Things had been different since Christmas. Not back to the total absentee Grace of the first couple of months Lenka had been there, but she sensed a subtle pulling back. Christmas dinner had been nice. Lenka had enjoyed cooking. It made her feel connected both to home and to her life here in Portland. It had been a good way to clear the decks of the Mackenzie fiasco. Grace had seemed tired, which was to be expected because of her long day at work, but she'd also seemed to enjoy the food and appreciate Lenka's effort.

So what had happened after that? Lenka wasn't sure. She had gone to a New Year's Eve party with Sue, which was fine. Grace had explained that she generally passed on celebrating New Year's. Her coworkers' kids were still off from school, and she liked to offer to work both New Year's Eve and Day because she didn't care about celebrating the stroke of midnight. So everything still seemed normal.

After school started again, Lenka was busier. School was going well, mostly. She was doing fine in all of her Portland State classes. She was also doing fine with her online course from her sending school, but she wanted to be doing better than fine. Simultaneous translation was the skill she needed if she wanted to work for the UN. It was easier in French than English, something coming to the US to study was supposed to help with. And it had, especially the volunteer hours at the hospital. That had hugely increased her vocabulary, mostly in a health-related direction. That wasn't exactly what she needed if she was going to translate for the UN. But the scope of what the UN discussed included healthcare. There'd been a recent UN general assembly high-level meeting on tuberculosis, for example. She needed to be proficient overall.

If that was what her goal still was.

Meanwhile, she and Grace had continued to cohabitate nicely. They'd hosted a few dinner parties together. It was all fine. Except that it wasn't. She and Grace had gotten to a level of comfortableness with one another before Christmas that just wasn't quite there anymore. Lenka had begun to hope for more, but instead, Grace had subtly pulled back. Lenka missed her and missed the hint of a possibility there could be more between them.

Grace was physically gone more, too. She'd mentioned a few dates. Lenka had no right to feel any sort of way about Grace dating, but she felt…something. Mostly, she just missed her, particularly the pre-Christmas version.

Meanwhile, there was school and homework and the hospital and friends. One of those friends, Carson, whom she'd met in Topics in Lesbian and Womxn Identities in Literature the previous quarter was in another literature class with her this quarter. She'd suggested going to a coffee shop to study together, which sounded much better than studying alone at home on a Saturday when Grace was working.

They met at Lenka's local coffee shop. After placing her order with Willa, which involved the requisite light flirting, Lenka commandeered a table and started on her homework.

Carson came in a few minutes later, waved, and placed her order before joining Lenka. "Hey. What're you working on?"

Lenka held up the book to show the cover. "It's for my French seminar. It's a novel we're going to discuss."

"I wish I spoke a second language well enough to read a novel written in it."

It was a sentiment Lenka heard quite often from Americans. Some seemed to mean it more than others. Some were working on it. Others only admired the skill. Grace was in that category. She made Lenka feel like her skill was special. Until recently, she'd made Lenka feel special.

Lenka shrugged a little, never sure how to respond. "What novel did you choose for the literature essay?"

They went on to discuss the essay in question. Lenka was doing a lot of reading for school this year, which she was quite happy about. It meant that she wasn't doing as much reading for pleasure, but it was okay. Not everything assigned was good, but she was being exposed to things she never would have been at her sending school, which was very focused on language and translation. That only made sense, but Lenka was finding this broadened education interesting.

They passed several hours working together, sometimes quietly, sometimes talking things through, sometimes getting distracted with conversation. During one of the times they got sidetracked, Carson asked, "What're you doing this evening? Something with Grace?"

"No, she's working today, so she usually just comes home and crashes after that. Plus…" Lenka wasn't sure if she should go into the feeling that Grace was pulling back. Just a month ago, they might have planned on dinner together once Grace was home, followed by watching something until Grace fell asleep on the couch, and Lenka covered her with a blanket. Or held her in her lap like that one time. That seemed far in the past with how things were lately.

Last night, though, Grace had said she was packing a dinner to eat at work if she had the chance because she was planning on coming home and going straight to bed. She was going for a hike the following day with someone named Jen. It was none of Lenka's business, but she was a little sad that it wasn't her whom Grace was hiking with. Last month, she was pretty sure it would have been.

"Plus what?"

Lenka shook her head. "Nothing, really."

"Well…if you're free, do you want to do something? Maybe go dancing?"

Lenka thought back to going to the club with Mackenzie. It had been fun for a while, but she wasn't sure she wanted to go again. Her mind flashed on an image of holding Grace close while they danced. She wondered if that was something Grace ever did. Not since Lenka had been there. At least, not that she knew about.

Maybe she had recently. She'd been out a lot. But Lenka thought not. Grace loved being around her friends and loved it when they all went home, too. She couldn't imagine her being happy in a sweaty crowd like that, even with the image of them dancing together still playing in her head.

"Or we could do something else if you're not into dancing. See a movie? I mean, now that you don't have a girlfriend anymore…"

Carson was asking her out on a date. Did she want to go on a date? She should have wanted that. She hadn't been heartbroken about Mackenzie, so it wasn't too fast to move on. And she wanted a girlfriend. That was what she'd liked best about being with Mackenzie, having a real girlfriend, even though it had turned out she wasn't her real girlfriend. But Lenka had enjoyed feeling chosen and special to someone.

In Louny, she hadn't felt exactly ostracized but also hadn't felt very welcome in her small town where she seemed to be the only queer person around. France had been easier, but that was still in a small town where there hadn't been a lot of opportunities for dating. Once she'd moved to Prague, she'd had some dates here and there, but nothing had stuck. So now that she was free of Mackenzie, she should have been dying to get out there. But something held her back, so she told a little white lie. "I think maybe it's too soon for me."

Carson gave her what seemed to be a genuine smile with just a hint of tightness. "No problem. We could just go as friends?"

"I'd love to. But maybe another time?" She was ready to go home and cook dinner. For herself. But enough to share should Grace come home hungry because that was just a nice thing to do. And she didn't feel like going out after. She felt like cuddling with Loki if she couldn't cuddle with Grace.

"Yeah, sure." Carson started gathering her things. "I should get going."

Lenka hesitated for a moment, then put her hand over Carson's. "I mean it. I do really like hanging out with you. I'd love to hang out more. But my finances are feeling pressed after having Mackenzie in town, and I'm hesitant to spend more money right now." That really was true. She realized as she said it that it was definitely part of why she'd said no. "But maybe you could come over for a movie at my place tomorrow afternoon?"

Carson's eyes cleared. "Yeah, okay. That would be great. Will, um, Grace be there?"

Lenka treaded carefully. She wanted Carson as a friend, but she wasn't interested in dating her. For reasons she wasn't clear on. "I don't know for sure. I think she has plans. She might be around part of the time. Loki definitely will be." She laughed. "We could invite some others, make a get-together of it? Or a one-on-one friend date. Whichever you like."

"Let's have a friend date movie viewing." Carson settled back into her seat, pausing the hurried gathering of her things. Lenka hoped that meant she was okay with the line Lenka was drawing. Carson tilted her head slightly. "So, as your friend, what are your future plans now that you and Mackenzie broke up? Am I going to get to come visit you in New York? Prague? Or are you staying here?"

"Yikes, Carson. Way to put a girl on the spot." It was a figure of speech she'd overheard recently and had been looking for an opportunity to use it. While the sentiment was apt, she was also pleased to have found the moment. She threw her hands in the air for the dramatic effect. "Ugh. I wish I knew."

"Okay, but what way are you leaning?"

Lenka bit her lip. "I seriously don't know. I'm still drawn to the idea of working for the UN, but I love my time at the hospital, and I love Portland. I feel like I'm building something here, you know?"

Carson nodded. "You totally are. Me, for example."

And Sue. And the friends she'd met through Grace. Those people made Lenka feel like she had a community, but it was more than that. It was what she was learning at school, her work at the hospital, and Grace.

Grace was in a different category for her, but maybe she shouldn't be. Grace was her roommate, and lately, it seemed that was all she wanted to be. She had plenty aside from Grace to anchor her here, but she still wondered what was up with her these days.

Chapter Twenty-two

When Grace got home from work, she smelled dinner. Again. And yet again, she ignored her better judgment and followed her nose to the kitchen where Lenka was cooking enough for two, even though Grace had told her she was going to eat at work. And yet again, Grace said, “Yum, it smells really good in here.”

Lenka turned to her with a welcoming smile. “Have a seat. It’s almost ready.”

Grace felt like an asshole. She kept pulling away while Lenka kept reaching out. Who did that? What kind of friend was she? She could go on dates and still show up as a friend for Lenka, even if so far, all she could think about on her dates was how much more fun she’d be having at home. She was a mess and needed to get her act together.

So this evening, even though she’d planned on going straight to bed after they ate, she said, “Want to watch a movie?”

The way Lenka’s face lit up made Grace’s stomach swoop in a way she’d yet to feel with any of the three dates she’d been on in the last few weeks. She’d put out the call with her friends that she was ready to be set up. Several had suggested people before, so they were eager to follow through.

She’d gone to dinner with one woman, who was nice enough until she got a call from an ex in the middle of dinner and took it. Needless to say, no second date.

The second woman, someone Carissa knew from school, showed up for a hiking date in flats. Grace had felt stupid to be in her hiking shoes with a backpack full of layers and lunch. She'd left it in the trunk and shifted gears. They'd walked the paved paths at Laurelhurst Park instead of going to hike in the Gorge like Grace had planned. It was okay that they'd gotten their wires crossed about that, but the crossing wires continued through the date. Grace felt like they were talking past each other no matter how hard she'd tried to get on her wavelength. Also no second date.

The third, a friend of a friend of Greg's hadn't shown up until half an hour past their meetup time. Grace had just put her coffee mug in the bin and was heading for the door when the woman had strolled in wearing the flowered skirt she'd told Grace she'd be wearing. She was beautiful, curvy, and confident, but Grace had resented her confidence when it meant she was breezing in so late. She'd just walked up and suggested they order. Grace had opted to stand up for herself and say she was leaving. She'd have stayed if the woman had shown any signs of regretting inconveniencing her, but no. She didn't have time to waste like that and couldn't see a future with someone who didn't bother to show when they said they would.

It was worse than the roommate search. Okay, maybe not because there wasn't a financial catastrophe hanging over her head if she didn't find a girlfriend.

What she did have hanging over her head was Lenka. Or more like, Lenka had taken up residency in her head. After or even during each of the dates, Grace had found herself comparing them to Lenka, who had more than once declined a call when the two of them were hanging out. She and Lenka were able to have conversations and tease without issue. Lenka had never been late when they'd had plans.

No, that wasn't true. One time, Lenka had messaged to say she'd gotten held up, and she was sorry. They'd both been working at the hospital that day, and Lenka had offered to just take the bus so as not to inconvenience Grace. But of course, Grace had waited.

Maybe tomorrow's date would be different. It was with a friend of Maci's, Jen, who'd just moved to town. Maci had grown up in a small town in Oregon and had moved to Portland for college and stayed for work. Jen had recently decided that Beachside, while incredibly scenic, was not exactly a lesbian dating haven, and she'd moved to Portland. She'd taken a teaching position with Portland Public Schools that had become available midyear. She had visited Portland a few times before and had actually come to one of Grace's dinner parties last year. She'd liked her.

But while sitting here having dinner with Lenka and watching a movie, Grace felt like going on the date was a betrayal of Lenka. Which was ridiculous. They were friends and roommates, and that was all they'd ever be. Lenka was here for a limited time, Grace reminded herself for the six hundred and first time. Plus, even asking her out was a violation of not only the exchange program's policy but of Grace's own moral code. It would be like a boss hitting on an employee. Friends was one thing, but asking her out was borderline harassment. If it was unwelcome, Lenka might not feel like she could say no without endangering her exchange.

So even as Lenka made a comment about the movie that sent Grace into a fit of laughter, she knew she was making the right choice. She needed to get over this crush by finding someone else.

❖

Having learned her lesson about planning a serious hike, Grace had suggested that they meet on Mt. Tabor for a walk. If Jen showed up in hiking shoes, there were trails that could take them for miles, but if she showed up wearing something else—say, high heels this time because why not—they could do just the little bit of incline to the top and around the tame, paved loop with views of the city.

Jen showed up on time, just a couple of minutes after Grace had parked, which was a green flag. When she stepped out of the car, she was wearing something similar to what Grace had on: leggings and a fleece jacket with the sort of shoes that might be running shoes and might be trail shoes. That was another green flag. Number three was her easy smile and enthusiasm when Grace told her about the different walking options.

It was around forty degrees and dry, which made it a good day to be out in Portland in the winter. They set out along one of the marked routes and started talking. It was a little stilted at first as they warmed up to each other, but pretty soon, they were bonding over stories of their cats.

"The first I knew of any of this was seeing her name pop up as a patient at the ED." Grace chuckled but shook her head, too. Now that there was some distance from the situation, she could see some humor in it, but at the time, it had been serious. She and Lenka were able to laugh about it together now, and that helped Grace not to feel too guilty. "Anyway, that's when we got to know each other better. I got sent home for a week because I'd been working too much overtime, and this brought me to my supervisor's attention. And Lenka needed some extra help."

"Luckily, my fluff has never maimed anyone beyond some scratches when she was a kitten. I think that pretty much tops the chart on cat hijinks."

"Right?" Grace spread her hands. "I win."

Jen laughed. "She seems pretty great. Lenka, that is. You got pretty lucky with getting her as an exchange student."

That launched Grace into the story of how she'd decided to find a student and how she'd thought she was getting a teenager. Jen was a good audience. She laughed at all the right places and asked follow-up questions. She made conversation easy. Grace was having a good time.

They kept talking over the course of the hour and a half walk. Grace was happy she wasn't the only one breathing hard on the steep inclines Tabor had on offer, but they both seemed into the hike.

"Would you like to get something to eat?" Grace asked as they neared their cars. "I could go for some lunch if you're up for it."

"Sure. You're the local, got anyplace in mind?"

"I had been thinking about going to a cart, but I'd like to sit inside and warm up." The hiking had made her sweaty in certain places, but her exposed face was feeling cold and a little chapped.

"I'm with you there."

There was a little back-and-forth before they settled on a taco place on Hawthorne. The conversation continued to flow. When they finally said their good-byes, it was with a hug and plans to have a second date. There was one moment where Grace thought maybe Jen was going for a kiss, but Grace wasn't feeling it and steered them to the hug.

As she drove home, she thought about that moment. Had Jen been looking for a kiss? And why hadn't Grace wanted to kiss her? Jen was attractive, good at conversation, and probably wouldn't become strange. After all, Grace had met her before, and Maci had known her most of her life. Grace had really enjoyed their time together and was looking forward to going to dinner and a movie in just a few days. It was all good, but kiss her? No. Not yet.

She probably just needed some time. She wasn't the fastest mover in the physical part of relationships, but that was mostly because she was never sure if she was making a new friend or dating someone. This time, though, she was sure about the dating, so holding back didn't make sense.

Or maybe she'd always been slow to transition to the physical in part because she was always slow to develop a physical attraction. That was probably all that was happening here. She'd probably be excited to hold Jen's hand at the movie.

Probably.

CHAPTER TWENTY-THREE

It seemed that Grace had a girlfriend, which was great. Lenka was happy for her. Grace deserved all the happiness. And she was acting more like the Grace that Lenka knew, so that was also great. In short, everything was great.

So why was she feeling so blue?

It probably had nothing to do with Grace. Lenka was in a good place right now, and if she could stay in the right now, she'd have nothing to be blue about. What was likely making her sad was not knowing what was going to happen in five short months. It wasn't like she didn't have some agency there, but she also wasn't sure what she wanted. Was the inclination to stay here in Portland a knee-jerk desire to cling to something familiar when the past year had been all about change?

She'd gotten a girlfriend, sort of. She'd moved to Portland when she'd expected to move to New York. That move had taken her away from everything familiar in Czechia. She'd taken classes unlike any she'd ever taken before, classes that had broadened her mind. She'd made new friends, some of whom felt more like family than some of her family. She'd be friends with Sue for the rest of her life, she was sure. And Grace, of course. She'd broken her arm and started volunteering at the hospital. She'd broken up with her sort-of girlfriend. It was a lot.

Now that she'd adjusted to all of that change, it only made sense that she'd want to cling to this new normal rather than start over in New York. But did that mean she shouldn't take the risk and try for the UN, which had been her dream ever since starting her translating program? She just didn't know.

On Christmas Eve, she'd been sure that her future was here in Portland. Between the strange end to her relationship with Mackenzie—they'd said they could be friends but hadn't talked since that day—and her realization that Grace's house and the people in it felt more like home than anyplace in Czechia, she'd been sure that was where she belonged. It had been an overwhelming feeling.

However, with a little distance, rational thinking, and the odd hot and cold coming from Grace, she wasn't so sure. Not sure enough to throw away her long-standing dream of translating for the UN.

The smart thing to do was to throw herself into her studies. She'd struggled a little in the fall term because of the need to ramp up her English to upperclassmen level. She'd ended up with decent grades, but this quarter, her goal was excellent grades, especially in her translating course. She was spending long hours practicing. She had to send in a recording of her simultaneous translations, and she spent hours doing it again and again until it sounded perfect. She had long study dates with both Sue and Carson.

One Sunday, when Grace was off work and out with Jen, she went from a morning coffee and study session with Sue to an afternoon session with Carson. Well, she didn't go anywhere. She sat in the coffee shop, buying an occasional cup to justify using the table for so long.

"You look like you've been here awhile," Carson said as she slid into the seat Sue had occupied half an hour before.

"She's been here for hours," Willa said. She was wiping down the table next to Lenka's and had been giving her a hard time about all work and no play. "You should make her go for a walk or something. I'll make sure no one takes the table. Just leave your stuff."

"She's right," Carson said. "I heard on a podcast recently about how you should walk for five minutes every half an hour. I know it sounds like a lot of interruption, but apparently, it makes you more productive in the long term. Let's at least go around the block. It's not raining right now."

It was February, which seemed to mean that it rained more often than not in Portland. Carson was right. She should really stretch her legs. She felt a little muddled and over-caffeinated at the same time.

This was why it was good to have different types of friends. Sue would never have suggested they take a break from their studies. She had a serious work ethic and thought studying was more important than…well, most everything.

Carson, on the other hand, was into a lot more life balance, something she reminded Lenka of as they walked down a side street into the neighborhood. "What's gotten into you lately? You've turned me down for a movie night twice this last week and are still plugging away. Are you really that far behind?"

"Um." She wasn't behind at all. She was, in fact, currently reviewing vocabulary words she knew by heart.

"What? Is it that bad? Do you need help?"

"No, I'm not actually behind." She shoved her hands in her pockets. She'd left her gloves at the coffee shop.

"Then why all the work?"

"I just want to do really well this term."

"And what do you mean by well?"

"Um…A's?"

"Is that a question?"

"Yes?"

Carson bumped into her. "Come on. What's going on? Because it's clear that there's something going on besides feeling studious."

Lenka sighed. "I want to do well so I have options, but I'm not sure what I want those options to be. Also, I'm working really hard, but I seem to have lost the joy of learning that I had last term." She'd had no idea she was going to say that. She hadn't even known that was how she was feeling until the words came out of her mouth. She'd thought she was doing a good thing, buckling down. "Shit." She blinked back tears.

Carson stopped and took her arm. "Okay. Deep breath. What options are we talking about here? Where to live? Job?"

Lenka threw her free hand up. "Yes. All of that. Everything." There was more. She could feel it, even if she wasn't ready to face it. She wasn't the sort to get needlessly anxious, but she found herself just walking around with a ball of churning anxiety in her chest, and she didn't know why.

"Okay, okay. That's a lot. Everything is a lot. Maybe let's take it one piece at a time? What's got you feeling the most like crying?"

Grace.

At the unexpected thought, she stopped crying and started walking. Carson followed.

Grace had popped unbidden into her head, which was stupid. She and Grace were fine. They'd had a dinner party on Wednesday with what Lenka thought of as the hospital crew: Aubrey, Carissa, and Maci. Greg had been unable to come because of a library shift. Plus Jen. Who was a lovely person. They'd had a good time eating, talking, and laughing well into the night. Just last night, they'd watched a movie together after dinner. They were fine. So why was Grace popping into her head?

She couldn't say it when she didn't know why. And while she and Carson were doing fine as friends, she found herself thinking about when Carson had asked her out on a date. She couldn't tell her that the first thing that had popped into her head when trying to figure out why she was crying was another woman. Wait. She'd known she was interested in Grace as more than friends. The snuggle on the couch, the wiping of her chin, the way Lenka's thoughts turned to her at the drop of a hat, but to be in tears because of her indicated more than a little crush. Lenka had feelings for Grace. She was hurt that Grace was dating Jen. No wonder throwing herself into her studies hadn't solved anything.

Still, she couldn't get herself to say all that to Carson. "I don't know if I should stay here or go to New York." That was true. "That is, if I even graduate."

"Is there really a chance you won't?"

"There's always—no." She could be honest with herself about that, at least. She'd been building up the idea of maybe not passing to have something to focus on. "There really isn't. I just have to pass my classes, and I'm not in danger of not passing. However, I also have to pass the translator exam, and it's pretty grueling. The pass rate for my school is about seventy percent on the first go."

"Okay, so you'll graduate. And it sounds like your chances of passing the exam are good. Like, where are you in your class? Middling? Above average?"

Lenka wobbled a hand. "I guess a little above."

"Right. So you're good there." They stopped at a busy street. Carson looked at the sky. "Should we cross and keep walking or go back? It feels like the rain is going to start back up anytime."

Lenka followed her gaze. The clouds were looking foreboding. "Let's go back." They walked half a block before Lenka spoke again. "Okay, I'm going to graduate, and I'll likely pass. If not on my first try, then the second. But if I don't get an excellent score, I won't be qualified to work for the UN. They only take the best."

"I guess the question is, do you want to work for the UN? Like, still. I know it's been a goal."

Lenka put her hands back in her pockets. They weren't so cold now that they'd been walking awhile, but putting them in her pockets felt protective. She wanted to huddle into her oversized hoodie with the hood up. She wanted to be sitting on the couch at Grace's house under a blanket, watching the rain slide down the windows and sipping tea, preferably with Grace. Ugh. That wasn't happening, not when Grace had a girlfriend now.

"Yes and no. I love translating for the hospital, but I don't even know if they have an open position. Or I guess it doesn't have to be at Duniway. It could be another hospital, although one of their part-time translators said a lot of hospitals are moving to a remote gig model for translators. Meaning, they call someone on the phone to do it. I wouldn't like that much. I like being part of the action."

"Are you up for hearing my thoughts? I can just listen to you talk if you'd rather."

"No. I mean, yes, what do you think? I'm open to hearing. Maybe it'll make something make sense."

"Okay. What I'm hearing is a lot of enthusiasm about medical translating. I haven't heard that same enthusiasm when you talk about UN translating."

Lenka considered that. They walked in silence for most of the next block. They were nearly back to Alberta Street and the coffee shop.

Before she fully processed, Carson said, "Sorry if I overstepped."

"No, not at all. You're right. I love this job. I've been focused on the UN because it's glamorous, and I've wanted to live in New York, but I like it here. What's wrong with that? It's not wimping out if I've changed my mind, is it?"

"Not at all. People are allowed to grow or change their minds when they've been presented with new information. Clearly, you have been. You're trying something, and it's a fit." Carson shrugged. "Nothing wrong with that."

Lenka felt lighter. Not like all the weight had been lifted, but some of it had. She'd figured out what her ideal job was: full-time work as a translator in-person at Duniway. It was huge to know that. She might not get exactly that, but she could talk to Carissa and go talk to HR. She could also start looking at other hospitals. She could even look in other cities. Seattle was supposed to be great, too. Or what was stopping her from going to Vancouver B.C. or even New York after all?

Her brain shied away from those ideas, and she didn't stop to consider why. She knew she liked Portland. That was enough. She'd start here.

"Thanks, Carson. This has been really helpful." She held the door to the coffee shop open.

"You're welcome. Do you want to ditch studying and go get lunch instead?"

Lenka found that she did. That was, in fact, exactly what she wanted.

CHAPTER TWENTY-FOUR

Everything was going swimmingly with Jen, except for the fact that Grace still didn't want to kiss her. She wanted to want to. But she didn't actually want to. Holding hands was nice. She enjoyed spending time with her. It had only been a couple of weeks, but they'd had five or so dates. One of which was a group dinner at Grace's place. Jen fit into her friend group so well that it was like she'd been part of it all along.

Jen was exactly who Grace should have wanted to be with.

So why was she still pining over Lenka?

Lenka had been really cracking down on school lately, and Grace missed her. She shouldn't have. They saw each other daily. But it used to be that Lenka would do her homework at the kitchen counter while Grace cooked or with her laptop balanced on her knees while she sat on the couch next to Grace, who was doing no-homework things: playing games on her phone or reading or whatever. Now she was away studying all the time. Grace didn't begrudge her work ethic. Except she did.

And when Lenka was home, it was often while Grace was at work or off with Jen. Was that on purpose? If it was, Grace had no room to talk. She'd pulled away first and with good reason. She wasn't supposed to be pining over Lenka. It was why she'd put herself out there in the dating world. Why she was going to the Portland Art Museum with Jen this afternoon. Grace had mentioned that she wished she knew what to do with her bare walls, and Jen has suggested the trip so Grace could get an idea of what she liked. It was a great idea for a rainy Sunday afternoon.

Grace waited for Jen to pick her up while sitting on the couch on the deck. It was raining—more misting, really—and cool, but she had her coat on, and Loki was hanging out with her, so she was comfortable watching the hard-core Portland bikers go by. Her gaze settled on her problematic yard. She still wasn't sure what to do with it. She knew she didn't want a lawn to maintain. There were very few manicured lawns in her neighborhood. Portland was a city that tended toward overgrown lawns, trees dominating yards, and joyfully wild native plants with certifications to prove it.

But even by relaxed Portland standards, Grace's yard was an eyesore. There were dirt patches covered by dead viny weeds of some sort. Someone had once tried to get a flower garden going in one area, but now it was all tall brown stalks with a carpet of some green weed growing low to the ground.

How could she fix it? She knew nothing about gardening. She sighed. It was either leave the eyesore as it was, learn about gardening, or figure out how to pay for a professional landscaper to come in and do something with it. The reality of the cost of the latter ruled it out.

She pulled out her phone to see what books the library had on gardening. She hadn't gotten far when Jen's car pulled to the curb. Grace stuffed her phone in her pocket, opened the door to offer the warm and dry indoors to Loki—who deigned to accept—then jogged down the drive.

"Hi," she said as she slipped into the passenger seat.

"Hi." Jen smiled at her. "Ready for an arty adventure?"

"You know it. Although, art appreciation isn't exactly my strong suit."

Jen pulled away from the curb. "The joy of going to an art museum as a person who isn't in school is that you can decide for yourself what to appreciate. You don't have to know anything to know what you like."

"Nice. That does take the pressure off. I have to admit that I've never gone to the Portland Art Museum, not even on a field trip with school. Have you been?"

"I have. My AP English class took a multiday field trip to Portland to see various sights and go to some theater productions, so that was my first visit. But I kind of love it. I've been a bunch."

"That's cool, but why the art museum for your English class?"

"Got me. I think they were just keeping us busy during the day, honestly, and it was a good thing, too, because you should have seen the shenanigans we got up to when we had downtime." She proceeded to tell about all the mayhem of the trip.

Grace listened with interest. The bit about how two kids got themselves locked in a broom closet at one of the small theaters they went to was particularly funny, especially since one of them was Jen and the other was a girl who'd declared gay people gross until she'd engineered the closet thing. Jen was a good storyteller.

The problem was that Grace's mind wandered to a certain blue-and-green-haired woman—Lenka had put blue over her green after Christmas so it wouldn't be so holiday-ish—she'd last seen last night. She wondered what Lenka was up to today. When Grace had told her she was going to the museum today, she'd seemed interested, and Grace had wanted to invite her. Which was not a thing. One didn't invite one's roommate on a date. Well, sometimes people did. Doing things as a couple with friends was done. But maybe not quite so early in a situationship and certainly not someone Grace had feelings for.

Jen finished her story, and Grace made an appropriate response formed with the part of her brain that had been paying attention instead of dwelling on Lenka. They were nearly to the museum, so the hunt for a parking spot began. They got lucky and found one just a couple of blocks away. As they walked to the entrance, Grace took Jen's hand. Holding hands was a lovely thing, really. It said, "I enjoy you. I want connection. We're in this together." In this case, what they were in together was walking down the park blocks near the museum, but that was enough. This was working. At least working enough that Grace was happy to hold Jen's hand.

Grace paid since Jen had driven, and then they wandered. Grace found she enjoyed seeing all the art, but there was very little art that grabbed her attention. Jen seemed to get caught up in several of the paintings, standing and staring at them for quite a while. When that happened, Grace would roam the room, looking briefly at each work. She wondered idly which ones Lenka would like. Would she like this one of Mt. Hood? Maybe they should go to the Saturday market when it opened back up and pick out some artwork together for their house.

Their house. No. It was Grace's house, and Lenka would soon be gone. In the middle of the date with Jen, she was having to remind herself of that fact.

"Do you like this one?"

Grace started. She hadn't realized that Jen was right behind her as she'd been looking at the painting and letting her mind wander.

"Oh, um, yeah. I think I like the subject more than the style, though. I was just thinking that maybe some pictures of Portland and Mt. Hood would be cool to have on my walls."

"I like that. It seems very you." Jen took Grace's hand as they moved on.

They entered one room just as a family with whispering children left. They were alone. Jen squeezed Grace's hand. Grace smiled at her. Jen leaned in.

Grace leaned back. She didn't mean to.

Jen cocked her head. "Are you…do you consider this a date?"

"Yes. I'm sorry. I'm not sure what happened. I like you, Jen."

"But you don't want to kiss me." Jen said it without the inflection of a question.

"I, um." Grace hung her head. "No."

"Are you on the ace spectrum?"

Grace's head snapped up. "What? No. I mean, huh. Actually, I'd never thought of it that way, but maybe. I have to really be into someone to want to…shit. I'm sorry."

"It sounds like you're saying you're not into me." Jen let go of her hand.

Grace kept her hand out for an awkward moment, then let it hang by her side. "I'm sorry. I mean, I really do like you. And I want to want more, but I think it's friendly feelings only."

Jen crossed her arms. "Why didn't you just say so?"

"I really, really wanted to want to date you. God, that sounds horrible. I'm so sorry."

"Why did you want to so badly?"

"Well, a lot because you're great. I really do mean that. I'm so glad I've gotten to know you."

Jen's face softened a little. "But that's not all."

"No." Grace looked down again. "I've been trying to not be into someone else."

"Is it Lenka?"

Grace looked back up. She might as well have been nodding for how much her head was moving. "Oh my God. Am I that obvious?"

Jen chuckled. "Yes and no. I noticed you looking at her a lot at dinner the other night. I wasn't sure if it was just one of those best friend things or if it was more. I see it's more. Why don't you just date her?"

Grace turned to look at the Native American wood panel art as she answered. "I can't. For one, it's against the rules."

Jen stepped up beside her and appeared to examine the art as well. "Exactly what rules are we talking about?"

"The exchange program rules."

"What?"

"Lenka is my exchange student officially."

"Wait. You're hosting her? And there are rules? She's not just your roommate while she's here going to school?"

"Exactly." Grace moved on to look at something else. She explained how it had all happened as they roamed. "So one of the rules of the program is no dating your exchange student. Which makes total sense. There's an inherent power imbalance."

"For most people. But she's, you know, older than you and can certainly make decisions for herself."

Grace conceded the point with an incline of her head. "Yes, but still. It'd be wrong of me to ask her out. If there were to ever be anything, she'd have to initiate. Otherwise, it puts her in an awkward position."

"So you're just hanging around waiting for her to ask you out?"

"No, of course not." Grace shot her a grin. "I'm dating people to get her out of my mind."

Jen actually laughed at that, which made Grace feel better about the whole situation. It seemed they might come out of this as friends. "And how is that working out for you?"

"Not awesome. You see, I've gone on a few dates with this awesome woman, but I'm not really available, which is shitty of me, and I hope she forgives me."

Jen elbowed her lightly. "Already done."

Grace drew a hand across her brow. "Whew."

"Seriously, though, you're just waiting on her to want to date you?"

"No. Even then, I don't think I should get involved. She's only here until the end of the school year."

"Hmm. Are you sure about that?"

Aubrey had said something along those lines, too, but Lenka's plan had always been New York. "As far as I know. I'm not excited to date someone when there's a clear expiration date." Grace pointed at a new room. "Look at that. They've got *The Wave*. Even I know about that one."

They went into the Asian art room, and the conversation turned away from Grace's pathetic crush and on to the art. After they'd had their fill, they stopped for dinner before Jen dropped Grace off. As had happened at the end of each of their dates, they hugged. This time, though, they were both clear it was a friend hug.

"I'm sorry about the not being present for dating thing," Grace said. "I really didn't mean to lead you on or anything. I really was trying to want to date."

Jen squeezed her shoulder. "Don't worry. I wasn't exactly head over heels over here. We can do the sensible sapphic thing and shift to friendship."

Grace put a hand on her chest. "While I am mortally wounded that you weren't that into me, I'm also glad. I'd feel horrible if I'd hurt you. Friends it is. Come to dinner again next weekend. Lenka is inviting a few friends, and so am I."

"I'm honored to be among them." Jen winked. "See you then."

Jen drove off leaving Grace standing in front of her house. She stared at it, her home and Lenka's, at least for now. Her plan to get Lenka off her mind hadn't worked. Maybe she should just lean in and enjoy her company while she was there. Not in a dating way but in a friendly way. Even if she never got to hold Lenka's hand, spending time with her as a friend was still time well spent. Once she was out of the house, Grace could consider dating again and maybe really get over her.

She squared her shoulders and walked in.

CHAPTER TWENTY-FIVE

Good morning." Grace smiled at Lenka over her coffee mug. "What do you have going today?"

Lenka's return smile was big and automatic. She and Grace had been in a good groove the last couple of weeks. Or maybe it was Lenka who'd been in a groove, and that colored everything. Ever since her talk with Carson, she'd felt more settled, more clear-eyed about what her goals were, and more hopeful about her future. She'd spoken with Carissa about the possibility of getting hired on full-time at the hospital. Carissa had been excited about her interest but had also let Lenka know that there were complications and hurdles. While the hospital did sponsor visas for some employees, it wasn't super common. Also, Carissa wasn't HR; she was the volunteer coordinator. She didn't know if there were positions open for translators, nor if it was a position where Duniway was willing to sponsor a visa. What she had said was that she would talk to HR on Lenka's behalf and that she was cautiously hopeful about working something out.

Meanwhile, Lenka had taken a practice translator qualification test and had done well, so she had reason to believe that she'd pass the test. And she'd gotten so far ahead on her homework that she found herself with extra free time for a stretch.

That free time had been partially filled with spending time with Grace, who'd been present again in a way Lenka hadn't felt since before Christmas. They'd hosted dinner parties, gone on hikes, gone to the art museum together, and eaten dinner together pretty much every night for the last two weeks. It was great to have her friend back, even if they hadn't had any more "potentially more" moments. Lenka would have liked to explore the option for more, but friends was good. Friends was better than the post-holidays oddness.

"There's a little homework I should do, but that's about all the plans I have until we have to start cooking for this evening." They were having a handful of friends over for dinner. Well, maybe more than a handful. The list had been creeping up in numbers. They'd have to deploy leaves for sure. It was Maci, Greg, Carissa, Tess, Jen, Sue, Carson, and a couple of others.

"Oh, I forgot to tell you that Aubrey said she could come after all, so that's one more."

Lenka poured some coffee. "I thought she was working?"

"Yes, but she doesn't have to pull a double. Apparently, one of the doctors broke up with his girlfriend on vacation, came home early, and asked for shifts."

Lenka added almond milk, poured in a little sugar, and sipped to test the mix. It was good. "What? Not a medical professional hiding out by working?"

"Ha, ha. Very funny." Grace raised her mug, though.

Lenka smiled at the point scored. "Well, sounds like we've got a lot of cooking to do."

"True enough. I'm going to start some bread now and get some minestrone going in the Crock-Pot. I figure we're going to need it to supplement the lasagna with the numbers we've got tonight."

"Need any help?"

"Nah. We can do the salad and lasagna together later, but I've got this part. If you get your homework done while I'm doing that, maybe we'll have time for a movie or something before we need to work on the rest."

Lenka tapped her mug to Grace's and tried not to let her gaze linger. "Sounds like a plan."

She retrieved her stuff and set up at the table to work. She needed to finish an essay and write a whole other essay for a different class. Her in-person classes were all very writing heavy: reading and then writing response papers or essays, even for her French seminar. It was all very good for her language skills. She'd picked up a thesaurus at the same bookstore she'd found on her first day in town so she wasn't always using the same words. One could look these things up online these days, of course, but Lenka enjoyed having the book to flip through. Even more than that, she liked asking Grace's opinion and the discussions that sometimes followed.

"What's another word for explicit?"

Grace glanced up from where she was chopping vegetables. "Are we talking in a sex way or in a being very clear about what you're saying way?"

"A sex way." The essay Lenka was working on currently was for her literature class, and it was about references to sex in books of different eras. As soon as she said it, she felt her cheeks heat. Maybe this wasn't an appropriate question of someone she was crushing on who didn't seem to reciprocate.

"Lurid?"

She was in it now, though. "Isn't lurid kind of negative?"

"Yeah, I suppose that's true. What about graphic?"

"Maybe. I am talking about how much is actually said about sex instead of ignored or obliquely referred to."

"Descriptive?"

Lenka scribbled a few things down. "I like it. Any others?"

"Salty." Grace laughed as she added salt to the Crock-Pot.

"Really?"

"Really. Salty can also mean something like racy."

"Huh. I thought it meant something like, you know, when a person is speaking up for themselves but in a grumpy sort of way, they're being salty."

"Yeah, that, too and much more commonly. Salty for racy isn't super common, but I've heard it. Language is odd, right?"

"But so very cool."

They worked, occasionally talking, for nearly two hours. By then, Lenka was done with the one essay and had a first draft of the other. Grace had the bread formed and on its second rise. The soup was on its way, and the dishes were done.

Grace slid into the seat across from Lenka. "Well? How's the homework going?"

Lenka shut the laptop decisively and started gathering her things off the table. "I'm done. For now, at least. You said something about a movie?" She could start editing the essay, but she'd much rather watch a movie with Grace, even if it wasn't quite noon yet.

"The next on the list?"

After their Christmas movie extravaganza, they'd had a few weeks in which they weren't watching movies, at least not together. When they'd started watching again—during the time where Grace was around once more but not really there-there—they'd watched a few movies here and there without a theme. A couple of weeks ago, they'd decided on a new movie project. They were watching all the movies listed on a Valentine's movie list and ranking them. Some had been really fun, others eye-rolling stupid. Some were repeats for one or both, but they were watching the entire list, no exceptions. Valentine's Day had already passed, but that didn't stop them from continuing their self-assigned task.

"Yes. I'll do snacks, you queue up?"

They settled in to watch Sandra Bullock bribe her underling into marrying her. There were a couple of stupid moments that had them making snide comments, but overall, they both really liked it.

"I mean, Sandra Bullock. It's hard to go wrong. I could look at her all day," Grace said when the movie was over.

"It would have been improved with a female romantic interest, but aside from that, top marks."

Grace jabbed a piece of popcorn she'd just fished out of the bottom of the bowl at Lenka. "Exactly right." She looked at her phone. "We probably have time for another…"

Lenka checked her own phone. "Maybe we should go assemble the lasagna and bake the bread, then come back?"

Grace sighed a theatrical sigh. "Fine. Be responsible."

When their friends started showing up, the second movie was done, the food was in the process of being put on the table, and Lenka was in an excellent mood. She was having such a great day, and it was only better with the addition of friends. More friends. Grace was obviously a friend, too.

Once everyone was there except Aubrey, who would join them as soon as her shift was over, they sat down to eat to murmurs of appreciation. Lenka was sitting at the opposite end of the table from Grace. Her particular friends were sitting with her, talking about how the term was going for each of them. With quarter terms, things went fast. It was the end of February, which meant that midterms were already behind them, and they were well on their way to finals in about a month. Lenka was listening and contributing, but she was also very aware of Grace. She kept hearing her voice and laughter that had her gazing down at the other end of the table. Many of the times she looked to Grace, she found Grace looking back at her. When their gazes met, warmth spread though her chest.

"Excuse you," Carson said.

"What?" Lenka asked.

"You have heart eyes. Are you into Grace?" Carson had the grace to keep her voice down. Sue was talking to another exchange student on her other side, and no one seemed to be paying attention to them.

"What?" Lenka was the one who drew attention with her loud reply. Grace looked at them with a questioning half-smile. Lenka shook her head a little and slid her eyes away. *Nothing to see here.* She modulated her voice. "No. Of course not. She's a really good friend. And roommate. I'm not into her." She didn't know why she was lying. Except that it seemed that Grace only wanted to be friends. Admitting aloud that she wanted more felt bad.

"Sure. Because that little display was super convincing."

"Seriously. She's my host mom, for crying out loud." But like the last time Lenka had joked about Grace being her mom, she'd felt the ick for having said it.

Carson scoffed. "You two in no way, shape, or form have any semblance of a mother-daughter relationship. You never have. I thought you were, as you say, good friends before. But seeing you tonight, there's more there. And she stopped dating Jen, right?

You've been in a much better mood since then. It all makes sense. You've got it bad for Grace."

Lenka glanced at Grace and away. She leaned in and whispered, "So what if I do? She just wants to be friends."

Maci leaned across Carson and said, "That is not true."

"What?" How could it not be true? Grace had just been dating Jen. She'd very clearly chosen to date other people, even after Lenka had broken up with Mackenzie.

"She thinks it'd be inappropriate since she's your host and whatever."

"Why would it be inappropriate? I'm not a teenager or anything."

Maci gave an exaggerated shrug, knocking her shoulder into Carson. "Sorry."

"No worries," Carson said, sounding like she was watching the best show. "Please continue."

Maci smiled at her. "I know, right? These two." She turned her attention back to Lenka. "She's super into you, but you're going to have to make the first move."

Lenka was so surprised and delighted about the possibility that she reverted to Czech.

"You seem gobsmacked," Carson said. "Are you okay?"

"Gobsmacked?" Even in this moment of shock, Lenka was distracted by a term she hadn't heard before. That was twice today, with salty and gobsmacked. It happened so rarely these days and now twice in one day. Was the ground even solid under her feet?

"Yup. Like something smacked you upside the head and left you without your wits."

That was how Lenka was feeling. How could she have been in love—yes, love. The feeling of home, the jealousy when Grace was dating Jen, the way that even with the distraction of their friends around, Grace shined for her. It was love. How could she have been in love and willing to just let it pass by because she didn't understand Grace's position? The realization left her gobsmacked.

It was her new favorite term.

"I…I think I need to…" Lenka pushed her chair back. Grace's head snapped up. Lenka stared at her. Grace looked curious and concerned, but there was more in that look. Lenka wasn't sure what exactly it was. She couldn't think. She turned and fled.

She found Loki hiding in her room. He didn't love company and usually hung out in one of the bedrooms when people were over. It used to always be Grace's room, but now it was Lenka's room sometimes. He raised his head in what she took to be alarm when she first entered, but when he saw it was her, he settled back down. When she sat next to him and stroked his silky back, he purred.

"I'm not sure what to do, Loki." She leaned over and whispered in case anyone was listening in. "I think maybe I love your mom."

He began to knead her bed cover.

"I know. It's big. But does she really feel the same? Should I go for it?"

He rolled onto his side, and she complied with his unspoken request to stroke his side.

"It's against the rules, and I guess that's important to your mom. But we're not exactly in the typical exchange student and host situation. I don't know that those rules apply to us. We're more like roommates."

He turned onto his back. She knew it was dangerous, but she stroked his belly. It was so soft.

"Should I ask her out? But what happens at the end of the exchange? What if I don't get a job and can't stay?"

He sank his claws into her arm.

She gasped in pain and withdrew her hand. She knew she'd been playing with fire there. And damn if that wasn't an apt metaphor for asking Grace out. She'd be jeopardizing the friendship they had. And if Grace did say yes, if Grace—she didn't dare believe it—loved her, too, then she'd be adding a huge additional pressure on to the already pressure-filled need to get a job. And she'd already planned a future around someone she'd thought was her girlfriend. Did it make sense to do that again?

There was a knock at her door.

"Come in." She wasn't sure whom she expected. Carson, maybe. She'd left that conversation abruptly.

It was Grace with a look of concern. "Are you okay?"

"I…" She didn't know what to say now that she knew she was in love with her. All the ease between them was just gone. "Yes. I just…needed a minute. I'm fine."

"You're bleeding. Did that little devil cat injure you again?"

Lenka looked at her arm. Sure enough, there was blood. Loki had gotten her good. He was still lying there, looking interested in the fact that Grace had shown up, but otherwise like he didn't have a care in the world. He probably didn't. Maybe he didn't even remember his bid to maim her. Lenka wished she could forget the past and move on as easily, to be so fully in the moment.

"Come on. Let's clean you up. We don't want you getting cat scratch fever." Grace chuckled at her own joke.

Lenka let Grace lead her to the bathroom. She still felt tongue-tied. She wasn't sure she could say anything in any language. Grace pulled the first aid kit out from under the sink. She had a small kit in each bathroom, plus a larger one in the kitchen. Lenka had been lucky if she had Band-Aids and a little antibiotic ointment in her apartment in Prague. It must have been a side effect of being a nurse to be so prepared for injuries.

"You're really quiet. Are you sure you're okay?"

Grace was bent over Lenka's arm, holding it gently, so Lenka was looking at the crown of her head. Her hair, while seemingly brown, was actually quite richly colored. There were natural highlights ranging from nearly blond to chestnut. The desire to run her fingers though it combined with the feel of Grace's fingers on her arm made her breath quicken.

Grace looked up. "Did I hurt you? I'm sorry."

"No…no. You didn't hurt me." Lenka pulled her arm back and pretended to examine the claw marks. "It's not a big deal."

"Okay, well, let the nurse decide that, please," Grace said with a playful tone. "This is going to sting a little." She poured hydrogen peroxide onto a cotton ball and dabbed the wounds. Lenka hissed. It did sting. Grace gave her a sympathetic look. "That part is done.

Now a little ointment and a Band-Aid, and you're all set." She worked quietly for a moment. "Did something happen?"

"Besides Loki clawing the shit out of me?" Lenka was deflecting, and she knew it.

"Yes. You rushed away from the table before that."

"It was nothing." It had been everything, but Lenka wasn't ready to talk about it. Now, while there was a tableful of guests in the house, was not the time. She wasn't entirely sure there was going to be a time. She wanted there to be, but the circumstances weren't ideal. And she wasn't about to repeat past mistakes.

"Okay." Grace gave her a doubtful look but didn't push. "I'm going to get back out there, then."

"I…"

Grace looked at her expectantly.

"I'll be right behind you," Lenka said, feeling foolish.

Grace patted her shoulder. "Okay."

Lenka watched her go, wanting to call her back.

Chapter Twenty-six

When Grace returned, Aubrey had arrived. Her hair was damp, and Carissa was giving her shit for not having her hood up in the rain. Grace slipped back into her seat and chimed in, "Getting cold and wet will get you sick."

"Oh please," Maci said. "We're medical professionals. Please tell me none of you really believe that."

"It's true," Sue said from the other end of the table. "Everyone knows not to go outside with wet hair."

"I didn't, I'll have you know," Aubrey said as she dug into the food on the plate Carissa had just handed her. "My hair was dry when I left the building. It was on the walk to the car and from the car to here that it got wet."

"No, I don't really believe that," Grace said to Maci. "I mean, it's true that if you've been exposed to something, being cold can make it more likely it'll take hold, though."

"See?" Sue said. "True. Also, you shouldn't drink anything cold if you're sick."

That started a discussion about the merits of that idea. The mix of medical knowledge versus cultural beliefs was an interesting area for the whole table, and the conversation wandered down those roads for a while.

Grace got up to get a new bottle of wine. When she turned back, Tess was standing there. "I was wondering if, now that you're in a place to be dating, you wanted to try again?"

"What do you mean?" Grace's mind wandered to Jen. No, she didn't want to try again. It hadn't worked.

"I just mean that, now that you're dating, we should try again. You said you weren't in a good place to date before."

Grace felt ashamed. She'd told a white lie when she'd said she just wanted to be friends with Tess, or at least, she'd thought it was a white lie at the time. Now it was coming back to haunt her. She was going to have to fess up. "I, um, really think we're better off as friends."

"Oh. I thought…what with inviting me tonight…Grace, I don't want to be friends with you. I'm going to go."

Grace didn't know what to say to that. If Tess wanted to date or nothing, then it would be nothing. She wanted to tell her not to go, but what right did she have to ask her to stay? "If that's how you feel."

"It is." Tess looked defeated, but she also didn't make a move to leave.

Grace refrained from saying something she'd regret later, like, "Maybe someday."

The silence stretched. Lenka returned, and Grace's gaze went to her.

"I see how it is," Tess said. She finally left.

Lenka gave Grace a curious look. Grace shrugged as she came back with the wine.

"What's up with Tess?" Maci asked when Grace sat.

"Apparently, she thought the invitation to dinner meant more than it did."

Maci shook her head. "She's never fit in." She shot a quick look at Lenka, then back at Grace.

It was true enough. Tess had never fit in like Jen did or like Lenka had from her first dinner party. She was a little annoyed that Maci was not being at all subtle with her opinion. What if Lenka noticed?

Grace wondered again what her leaving the table tonight was about. She'd seemed like she was having a good time until abruptly, she wasn't. But if she didn't want to share, she didn't have to. Even though Grace really wanted to know, even though Grace cared more about her short absence than about Tess having walked out of her life for good.

Carissa called down the table to Lenka, "I finally got an answer about the potential job." Grace's ears perked up. Was Lenka taking on a new volunteer position? Why hadn't she mentioned it? "HR says they want to keep you, and if paying you is the only way to do it"—there was laughter around the table—"they're willing to try to make that work." What? Lenka was looking for a job at Memorial? Her student visa didn't allow that, did it? "There's not exactly a position right now, so they have to figure out where the money is coming from and all that jazz, but your contributions are such that they're going to do what they can. And if they find the money, they're familiar with sponsoring visas and can do that. They'll have to jump through a few hoops, but they can. So fingers crossed, but it sounds promising." Carissa held up her crossed fingers to show she meant it.

"Wait. I thought you couldn't work for money on your student visa." Grace looked between Carissa and Lenka. Lenka looked like a deer in headlights. Carissa's expression was shifting from lighthearted and pleased to concerned and sheepish. What the hell was happening?

"Oh no, she can't. It was just about…" Carissa trailed off from whatever backtracking she was trying to do when Lenka held up a hand. The table went silent, watching things play out.

"It's for after," Lenka said. "I…I want to try to stay here. In Portland, I mean."

A torrent of emotions flowed over Grace. Surprise, of course. Relief came quickly. Lenka might not leave. Next was hope, but she quickly squashed that. Just because Lenka was staying didn't mean she was interested in Grace in any romantic way. A little hurt followed on the heels of the suppressed hope. Why hadn't Lenka told her any of this? Looking around the table, it was clear that Aubrey also knew, as well as Sue and definitely Carson.

Carson didn't look surprised at all. She was smiling at Lenka. That was probably why Lenka was staying, to be with her.

Grace shut down that line of thinking. Even if Lenka was interested in Carson, that was her business. But to assume that Lenka was staying for one particular romantic interest was quite the leap. Lenka clearly had a life going here. That was likely why she was staying. And if romantic interest in Carson was part of the rich tapestry that Lenka had woven for herself here in Portland, then Grace should have been happy for her. And happy that Lenka would still be in her life.

But she couldn't help the wave of jealousy that washed over her, accompanied by shame about the jealousy. "That's…that's great," she managed to get out.

"And of course, you need money. No one can live on ideals alone," Sue chimed in.

That started a discussion on the other end of the table about plans for after school and student loan debt and the like.

"I didn't know you didn't know," Carissa said softly. "Is it a problem?"

"No, of course not. I hope it works out."

Maci leaned across both Carissa and Aubrey to say, "I think our friend here is just stunned at the possibility that she could actually pursue a relationship with Lenka that wasn't doomed."

"Shh." But even as Grace hissed, she realized that she was probably drawing more attention that the softly spoken words. "There are a lot of assumptions in what you just said."

"Eh. I don't know. Which part?" Maci gave a cheeky grin.

Aubrey leaned over, too. "Because it's clear you're interested."

Grace put her hands over her face. She could feel her cheeks heat. "Even so, there's nothing saying that she—listen, this is a conversation best had when she's not sitting at the other end of the table." A quick glance between her fingers showed that Lenka was looking at her. She dropped her hands and offered a weak smile and a thumbs-up, then immediately felt stupid.

Greg leaned across the table, creating a little huddle of five at their end. Grace groaned to herself at the spectacle. "You should ask her out."

Grace glared accusingly at Maci. "Have you guys been talking about me?"

"We all have," Maci said cheerfully. "It's clear you're smitten. And Carissa was thinking if she got the ball rolling with the job—"

"Leave me out of this. I seriously thought they'd have talked about it, or I wouldn't have brought it up at the table." She paused. "That said, I agree. Ask her out."

"Dessert." Grace pushed back from the table and started collecting plates. "It's time for dessert."

Every pair of eyes at the table looked at her with varying degrees of surprise and curiosity.

"Dessert time," she reiterated.

Conversation slowly resumed as she walked to the kitchen. As she was loading dishes, she heard footsteps. Then, Lenka said, "I think it's my turn to ask if you're okay."

Grace straightened and took the plates from her with a smile she hoped wasn't forced. She was truly happy that Lenka wanted to stay in Portland. "I'm fine. That's exciting about the job."

Lenka looked at her as if she was trying to figure something out. "Really? Because you seemed a little gobsmacked." She said it with a hint of a smile.

"I, well, yeah. I was a little surprised. But I think it's great. Carson seems really happy."

Lenka looked at Carson, then back at Grace. "I suppose. I think she's happy because she knows it's what I want."

The fact that Carson knew but not Grace hit her hard again. She turned to the cake Carissa had set on the island earlier and busied herself with uncovering it.

"Grace?"

"Yes?" She didn't look up.

"Is something wrong?"

There was a little hurt in her voice, and that more than anything caused Grace to look up. "No. Really. I think it's great. I just wish I'd known."

"I…I didn't mean to leave you out. I just wanted to have more information before I shared."

"But everyone else knew." Grace knew it had come out bitter. She hadn't meant to be accusing, but it had just blurted out of her.

"Ah. Well, Carson was kind of there when I figured out it was what I wanted, and Carissa, well, that's who I needed to talk to about it. I didn't know that she was sharing with people."

"The gossip machine is strong at the hospital." Grace glared at her friends, all of whom turned away and pretended to be busy. Grace turned her back on them. "And particularly amongst them." She jerked her head toward the table.

Lenka copied her stance, leaning on the counter facing away from the table. "If this is because you are done with me as a roommate, I'm not assuming I'll still live here."

"You're not?" This time, hurt crept into Grace's tone. She was frustrated with herself. Why couldn't she just chill out? "I mean, you certainly don't have to. Are you and Carson—"

"No. I mean, I don't have other plans for where to live. But I'll find a place if you don't—"

"You're welcome here. Loki would miss you if you left."

A small smile appeared on Lenka's face. "He would, would he?"

Seemingly of its own volition, Grace's hand crept toward Lenka's along the edge of the counter. "He would. He doesn't want to lose his favorite punching bag." Was that her imagination, or had Lenka's hand shifted closer, too?

"And how does his mom feel about it?" There was something in Lenka's tone that Grace couldn't quite identify.

"I—" It occurred to Grace that she was no longer hearing conversation in the background. She looked over her shoulder and saw that the table had somehow emptied. "Where did everyone go?"

Lenka looked as puzzled as Grace felt. "No idea. That's strange."

Grace went to the living room. No one was there, either. Lenka passed her and looked out the window. "I think they're all leaving."

It only took Grace a moment to realize what had happened. She could play dumb, but what was the point? No, it was clear to her. Their friends had decided that she and Lenka needed time alone together. And how could they possibly be wrong about that? The two of them had been so wrapped up in their little drama in the kitchen that neither of them had noticed their friends slip out. That more than anything gave Grace the courage to believe that Lenka was feeling this, whatever this was, too.

She took her courage in her hands and turned. Lenka was still gazing out the window. The only light in the living room was from a lamp near the couch and the light shining through the open door to the kitchen. The soft lighting made Lenka's hair look like a darker green than it currently was. Grace wanted to feel the texture of it, let her fingers trace the shell of her ear. But she was still very aware of the fact that she should not make the first move. She was the host, the one with power between them. The most she could do was show her openness.

"That's so—" Lenka turned midsentence, and whatever she saw on Grace's face made her stop abruptly. "Oh."

Grace wasn't sure what she meant. She shifted a little and looked away, not wanting Lenka to feel any pressure. Lenka lightly touched her cheek, gently guiding her to face her once more. What Grace saw in Lenka's eyes this time, coupled with the touch, made her heart soar.

"Hi," Grace said.

"Hi," Lenka answered.

"So…you're staying?"

Lenka gave a slow nod, not breaking eye contact. "I want to. I'm trying to."

"Why?" Grace was nearly certain she knew what was happening, but there was a small part of her that wondered if Lenka was offering assurance of her continued friendship. "Not…I mean, not because of Carson?"

"No. Not because of Carson. Well, maybe a little." Grace's stomach dropped. "But only because she's a friend." Grace's stomach settled back in place. "I'm staying, or trying to, because I love my job, I love my friends, I love Portland, and I—I don't want to leave you."

"Oh." That was more than Grace could have dreamed. She was gobsmacked—the phrase was stuck in her head from Lenka saying it earlier—in the best way.

Lenka, who'd been looking serious and hopeful, began to look uncertain. "I'm sorry, was that…that was too much. I shouldn't have—"

"No!" Grace was a little too vehement in her attempt to stop Lenka's self-doubt. "I mean, no, it's not too much. I could understand why someone might think so. I mean, we've never even kissed or anything, but no. I feel the same. I just hadn't…I'm doing this all wrong." She was babbling. She took a deep breath and, encouraged by the way Lenka's eyes were shining, said, "I don't want you to leave, either." She wanted to say it was because she loved her, but if admitting they were into each other was borderline too much for never having kissed, then saying those three words was really too much. Besides, Lenka was trying to stay. It didn't mean she would. If Grace didn't admit to love, maybe it wouldn't be so bad if Lenka did have to leave. Her thoughts were spiraling into a resolution to step back, to retreat, when she noticed Lenka's reaction.

Her face had bloomed into a full-blown smile. "I think we should address the fact that we haven't even kissed."

Grace's desire to protect herself warred with the desire to throw herself at Lenka. The latter was winning, but there was one more stumbling block. "I know our situation is not a typical host family-exchange student deal, but technically, we're not supposed to date. And I don't want you to feel any pressure to—"

"The only pressure I feel is the driving need to kiss you. Grace, this is fine. You're right, we're not typical. I appreciate your caution and your clear communication that you aren't coercing me, but for crying out loud, please kiss me already." Lenka bit her lip, drawing Grace's attention to her mouth with her pink lip caught between her teeth. "Unless you don't want to. I also only am interested if you really want to kiss. No coercion."

"No coercion," Grace echoed in a whisper before she finally gave in and crushed her mouth to Lenka's.

Grace had imagined that Lenka's mouth would taste of the pomegranate-flavored lip balm she favored, but instead, she tasted slightly of garlic and tomato sauce from the dinner they'd just eaten. Grace wanted to devour her, and as they kissed longer, found that she tasted of something less like food and more like whatever Lenka's natural flavor was. It was a taste that drove her wild and had her wondering what other tastes Lenka's body had in store for her.

She'd expected to be turned on, and she was, but she also felt like she was melting into Lenka. A lightness in her chest at finally connecting with her in this way ballooned up, even while a heaviness in her belly grew with her want.

The feel of Lenka in her arms was precious to her, but also, Lenka was solid and pushing back with her own need. Grace found herself backed into the couch and then lying back with Lenka's small frame settling onto her. She welcomed the contact, pulling her even closer with a hand at the small of her back.

Grace's hips were moving, seeking. Lenka ground against her, then slipped a leg between her thighs. Grace wanted more and less. More pressure, more friction, but less between them. The jeans had to go.

She gasped at the thought. She'd never once had sex on a first date nor a one-night stand. Not because she was a prude. She had no problem with people who did those things, but she'd never wanted to. They'd never even had a date, and she wanted Lenka bare beneath her. And above her. She wanted them both bare.

Lenka pulled back. "Are you okay? Is this okay?"

"This is good. So good. Except, I think we should take it to a bedroom. That is, if you want to."

"Oh yes. I want to. Very much."

But instead of getting up, Lenka dipped her head and kissed Grace again. Grace kissed her back. She couldn't get enough of Lenka's lips, tongue, and teeth. She wanted more. Lenka kissed her way down Grace's neck, nudging her sweater aside to get to the space where her neck met her shoulder. Grace tilted her head to the side to give access and slid her hand under Lenka's shirt.

Lenka moved her hand under Grace's sweater and up her side. Grace moaned. Lenka returned to her mouth and swallowed her cry.

"Bed. Now. Please." Grace wanted more than she felt comfortable doing here with the front window open to the street. She pushed a little, and Lenka sat up. Her pupils had swallowed nearly all the green of her eyes, and the sight made Grace even wetter. She sat up and captured Lenka's mouth again.

Then, she was tugging on Lenka's shirt. Lenka lifted her arms, allowing her to remove it. She wasn't wearing a bra. Grace's mouth went dry, and she dipped her head to take one of her taut pink nipples into her mouth.

She'd been right. The taste of her was fantastic.

Lenka gasped and threaded the fingers of one hand through into Grace's hair. "I thought…bed?"

Grace's cheeks warmed when she realized what they were doing where any passing biker could see. "Yes, bed." She stood, taking Lenka with her. Lenka was small, and Grace was strong from moving patients around. She put her hands under Lenka's butt and carried her down the hall.

"You are stronger than I gave you credit for," Lenka said into her hair.

"I'm surprising myself, to be honest. Clearly fueled by lust."

"No complaints. It's very sexy."

Lenka's room was first, and Grace had no patience. Plus, light as Lenka was, Grace didn't know if she'd make it all the way to her room. She turned into Lenka's, squeezed her butt, and set her on her bed. She pulled her sweater over her head before lying on top.

Lenka's hands went to her back and undid her bra. "You forgot this."

Their jeans followed shortly after and were kicked to the side. Grace was torn between wanting everything right now and wanting to take it slowly. She returned to Lenka's breasts and mouthed her nipples until Lenka said, "Grace, please."

Grace could have demanded to know exactly what Lenka was begging for, but she wanted it just as much, so she kissed her way down Lenka's stomach to the top of her panties. She paused with her fingers hooked into the band. She knew she had Lenka's explicit consent, so it wasn't that. It was to savor the momentousness of the occasion. She wanted to see Lenka, to taste her, more than she'd ever wanted anything like this before. Her heart swelled with it. She was about to see all of the woman she loved, even if she couldn't say it, for the first time. It was a huge moment.

Lenka squirmed, and her hips gyrated. Grace took the hint and pulled the panties down. She was beautiful. Excitement surged. Grace pushed her tongue through the soft curls and finally tasted Lenka's center. Sweet, salty, and entirely Lenka.

Chapter Twenty-seven

The orgasm that ripped through Lenka under the ministrations of Grace's tongue felt like an out-of-body experience. Explosive pleasure had her arching off the bed and seeing stars. Grace's firm hands eventually brought her back to reality, and Lenka pulled her up to kiss her mouth clean of herself.

"That was amazing," she said when they parted.

"Good." Grace kissed the tip of her nose.

It was such a cute, sweet move that Lenka giggled. But even as she was luxuriating in the aftereffects of her climax, a different sort of drive was taking hold, and she began exploring Grace. She wanted to see her come apart with pleasure.

She slipped one hand into Grace's underwear to find her swollen and wet. Lenka groaned, and Grace pulled the underwear down, clearly signaling her desire. Lenka flipped them over and slid her fingers into Grace's folds. They moaned in tandem. Grace giggled. Lenka grinned and dragged dampness up to and around her clit. Grace threw her head back, and Lenka explored her exposed neck before working her way lower. She explored with hands and mouth, teasing, until Grace held her hand in place and thrust against her once, twice, before coming undone.

It was the sexiest thing Lenka had ever seen.

She settled against Grace, feeling cozy and satiated. Just a couple of hours ago, Lenka had realized she loved Grace. Now she was curled up against her, her curves a welcome resting spot.

Mostly. There was a part of her that wanted more. She couldn't help cupping one of Grace's breasts and playing a little.

When Grace's breathing evened out, she sighed. Happily, Lenka thought. Hoped.

"All good?" Lenka asked.

"So good," Grace said, but there was something in her tone that made Lenka think she wasn't being entirely truthful.

"Too much too soon?"

"No." Grace's tone was decisive. "It was amazing. Perfect." She put a hand under Lenka's chin and guided her into a kiss.

Lenka believed her. But there'd been something. "But?"

"I'm…in my head about the future."

Lenka nodded, chin moving against Grace's shoulder.

"I mean, if there is a future? I guess?"

"Of course there's a future. I mean, I hope so. I want there to be."

"Me too. But that'll be hard if you end up not in Portland."

"Yes. Agreed. I have no desire to have another long-distance relationship. Not that I…" Lenka stopped. She was still embarrassed by what had gone down with Mackenzie and hadn't shared that misunderstanding with anyone. It had been easy to hide because they didn't share any friends in common. It was another red flag. They'd never gotten to know each other's people, not even over video.

"Not that you what?"

Lenka wanted to be open and honest. She loved Grace. This was a new relationship but a well-established friendship, and the trust and emotional closeness had been built already. She rested her forehead on Grace's shoulder, which muffled her voice, but she was having a hard time looking Grace in the eye while she admitted, "I misunderstood what was happening between Mackenzie and me. She let me know on her visit that we'd never really been in any sort of relationship."

"What?" Grace's arms circled her, and she kissed her temple. "Oh, sweetheart. I'm sorry. That must have sucked. No wonder you were upset."

"Yeah." Her voice was still muffled. "I wasn't so much upset by that as by…well, I'm slow, it appears. Because that was the night I realized I was more at home here than I've been anywhere besides at my grand-mere's house."

Grace tightened her arms. "I'm glad, but why does that make you slow?"

Lenka raised her head and caught Grace's gaze. "Because I didn't realize it was about you until tonight. Once I knew, I realized it had been true for a long while now." She wanted to tell Grace that she loved her, but they'd only just admitted any feelings for one another. Throwing love into the mix *was* too much too soon. But she needed Grace to know that this wasn't some whim, some crush that had just occurred to her this evening that had her acting in haste.

Well, the acting on in haste might have been a little true. It had been a short bit of time from dawning realization to acting on it. However, it wasn't a fling or a whim. She loved Grace, and she wanted long-term. She wanted to be her girlfriend. But was that what Grace wanted, too? After all, she'd just been dating Jen, who was a lovely person. If she didn't go for Jen, would she go for Lenka? Maybe she was misunderstanding the whole situation. Again. Dread pooled in her stomach.

Grace smoothed it away, perhaps without even knowing it was there, by trailing her hand down Lenka's side and looking intently into her eyes. "Well, I knew I was…interested, let's say, way back in November. And it was obvious enough that Maci called me on it." She chuckled. "As for more, well, I think I had my first inkling of that when you came home so upset on Christmas Eve."

"All this time? We could have…" They could have been together for a couple of months, extending the clock on the possible deadline. But was that what Lenka would have wanted? To fall even more deeply in love with Grace only to leave? Her stomach felt tight.

Grace kissed her temple. "It wouldn't have been right. I couldn't have made a move. You were fresh out of a relationship. And…"

"And?"

"And I'm a rule follower. More than that, I think it's a smart rule. I never could have made the first move for fear I'd have been acting inappropriately."

Lenka pushed up on her elbow and kissed Grace softly. "You're such a good person."

Grace waggled her head dismissively, but she also had a small, pleased grin. "I can't tell you how thankful I am that you made the move."

Again, Lenka read hesitance. She was saying all the right things, but there was something that wasn't quite right. "But?"

"Ugh." Grace dropped her head back against her pillow. "How do you know me so well?" She took a deep breath. "I also didn't want to start anything because I knew you were going to leave, and what I know about myself now is that I'm an all or nothing person. I'm all in here, and I don't want a relationship where we're not both all in. I know that's a lot, and I didn't want to put that on you right now, but also it's how I feel, and I'm scared you won't be able to stay because even though you want to, it's not a done deal." She'd spoken the whole last bit in a rush, and now she looked away.

Lenka put a finger to her chin and pulled her back. "That's not too much, Grace. It's what I want, too. And maybe we should have waited, knowing that about ourselves, but I…I think we can make this work."

"Yeah? But if you have to leave…Never mind. We're here now. We shouldn't let any time go to waste."

Lenka could tell there was still hesitation. She felt it herself. She was so happy to be here, be with Grace, but if she couldn't stay, now that she knew Grace felt the same way—or maybe not love but maybe she could get there—it would be that much harder to leave. All she could do was try her best to stay. And Grace was right. They had now, and they should make the most of it. "We are here now. And I'm very glad."

Grace's eyes softened, and she pulled Lenka in for a kiss. The conversation was shelved in lieu of other activities.

Chapter Twenty-eight

A month went by in a haze of sex, cuddles on the couch, heart eyes, teasing from Grace's friends about said heart eyes, work, and only two dinner parties. With how much they liked hosting, two wasn't many in the span, but Grace, at least, had found it hard to open up their newly formed bubble of happiness. Besides, she still had work, and Lenka had school, so it wasn't like they didn't spend time apart and with others. They just, by unspoken agreement, spent all the time they could together.

One evening on the couch, Grace was scrolling through her social media feeds with one hand and massaging Lenka's feet where they rested on her lap with the other. Lenka was propped against the arm of the couch with her laptop open, typing away on some paper.

Lenka nudged her belly. Grace switched her attention to that foot. Lenka shifted the other against Grace's inner thigh and began a subtle movement.

"Listen, woman. You've got homework to do." Grace wanted to throw the phone and laptop aside and have her way with Lenka, but they'd been a little too into each other and Lenka too little into schoolwork. It was important to their combined futures that Lenka pass her classes.

"You are no fun when you're being the responsible one."

"It'll be no fun if you have to leave the country." The niggle of anxiety about what would happen at the end of the year squirmed its way to more prominence. Grace pressed a hand to her stomach to hold it in. She took a deep breath. It would be okay. Carissa said that Memorial was looking for funds and would likely find them. Lenka was passing her classes. It would work out. It would.

Lenka put her laptop aside and sat up. "Hey, hey. It's okay. I promise, I'm getting enough done. Most of my finals are essays, and I've already turned in three of the five. I'm not slacking. I promise. You're distracting, *kotě*, but not that distracting."

Grace pretended afront. "Excuse me, but who was late to class the other day because of my serious powers of distraction?"

One day last week, Lenka had sat up in bed clutching her phone. "Shit. I'm late for class."

Grace should have been paying attention to the time, too, but it had been one of her days off, and she'd been enjoying the lazy day, not completely sure what day of the week it was because she was so wrapped up in the small world of her bed. She'd only gotten up in the couple of hours they'd been awake to feed Loki and fetch food and beverages.

When Lenka had made her panicked pronouncement, Grace had hopped up, dressed quickly, and driven Lenka to school to save time. Now she was trying to not be so distracting, but it was hard when Lenka put her foot places.

Lenka put her hand on Grace's arm. "I swear, you don't have to watch out for me. I'm setting alarms for classes these days." She smiled a cheeky grin. "Also, I just finished this essay. Only one to go. And you know how I want to celebrate?" Her grin shifted into something hungry.

"Ice cream?" Grace asked innocently.

"Maybe later." Lenka climbed onto her lap.

Grace had to trust that Lenka had things in hand. She was a grown woman. Plus, how could she possibly think about holding back with Lenka in her arms like this?

Grace waited in the kitchen with two packed bags at her feet. She'd heard the door open and knew Lenka's arrival was imminent.

She had been out for brunch with her exchange friends. They were all taking it easy on this first Monday of spring break.

Grace was excited, with just a hint of nervousness. This was a surprise, and as with any surprise, there was the possibility that it wouldn't be as well received as she hoped. Loki was glaring at her from his hammock on the windowsill. He'd tried to prevent the packing by sitting on top of the suitcases, each in turn. She'd explained to him that Maci would check in on him every day, but he either didn't think that was adequate or didn't understand. It could have been either.

Lenka came in looking at something on her phone and started when she realized Grace was in the room. "Oh, hey, *kotě*. You scared me. What's up? Are those suitcases?"

"Surprise!" Grace threw her arms wide. "I'm taking you to the coast for a couple of days for spring break."

She waited nervously for Lenka's reaction and was relieved at her excited smile. She even hopped a few times. "Really? When did you plan this?"

It was a legitimate question, even if Lenka didn't realize it. Hotels on the coast during spring break were hard to find, even though the weather was unpredictable. It could be warm enough for kids to play in the water, or it could be raining and stormy. Either way, Oregonians flocked to the beach during the weeklong break from school. "I started looking shortly after That Night and just last week found two nights opened up." They'd been calling their first night together That Night, complete with capitals. "Someone must have canceled."

"Yay! Are we leaving now?"

"Yes, unless you want to check your bags. I think I got everything." Grace looked at the bags at her feet. She'd packed an outfit for each day, toiletries, and rain gear, although she figured that if the chance of rain materialized, they'd likely stay in and do indoor activities. That thought didn't exactly make her sad.

"I'm sure it's fine. Let's go." Lenka picked up one small bag, took Grace's hand, and headed for the door. She paused as they passed Loki glaring balefully. "Will Loki be okay?"

"He'll be fine. There's food and water out, fresh litter, and Maci is going to come by and love on him. If he lets her."

"Good. Okay. It's just that he looks so mad."

"Yeah, and he'll sulk for a little while after we get back, but it'll all be okay."

"If you say so," Lenka sounded doubtful, but she followed it up with a smile and a kiss.

Once they were in the car and on their way, Grace asked, "What does kotě mean, anyway?" She'd been meaning to ask for a while, but every time Lenka said it, she was distracted by something or another. Kisses, most often.

Lenka's laugh chimed out. "After a month you ask?"

"Well, you're rather distracting."

Lenka preened. "Kitten."

"Where?" Grace slowed, looking to see if a cat had run into the road.

"Kotě, it means kitten. It's a standard term of endearment in Czechia."

"Oh, so I'm standard, am I?"

"Not at all." When Grace glanced Lenka's way, she saw a blush on her cheeks. "You're the first person I've ever called kotě."

"Really? What did you call Mackenzie?"

"Zlatíčko."

"And what does that mean?"

Lenka laughed again. "It'll sound funny in English."

"Now I'm more curious."

"It means little gold, but we use it like you'd use honey, which would sound funny in Czech if translated literally. Anyway, I thought it was appropriate for Mackenzie because it was always important to her to shine."

Grace laughed. "I think I prefer kotě."

"It suits you."

"Now I'm offended. Do you think I'm homicidal like my cat?"

Another laugh. "No, I think you're cuddly and cute. And then there's your p—"

"Okay, okay. I get the picture." Grace laughed.

❖

"Excuse me, but are you hiding out at work again?" Maci stood, hands on hips, staring at Grace where she sat on the bench in the locker room tying up her work shoes.

"No," Grace said with as much dignity as she could muster, "I most certainly am not *hiding out*. I'm making myself scarce. There's a difference."

Maci sank onto the bench next to her. "Why? Are you and Lenka fighting or something? You didn't break up, did you?" She sounded aghast. "Because while you're my friend and all, I will slap you silly. She's perfect for you."

"Thanks for letting me know who not to tell should we ever break up." Grace shifted and shoved her regular shoes in her locker. "No. She's got her first shot at taking the official translator's test in a few days, and she needs quiet to concentrate on her studies."

"The first shot? There are more shots?"

"I guess there are indefinite shots? But if she doesn't pass by June, then she won't be certified in time to accept the job if it's offered, which means going back to the Czech Republic."

Maci leaned her head on Grace's shoulder. "If that happens, are you leaving me?"

Grace didn't answer. She didn't know the answer to that question yet, but she'd begun to consider the possibility that if Lenka couldn't stay, Grace could move. Maybe even to Prague. She'd looked a little at the possibility of getting a visa before slamming her laptop shut because she was too overwhelmed to sort it out.

Maci stiffened. "I was joking, but are you?"

Grace sighed. "The thought has crossed my mind. But I'd really rather not. I want to stay here. I love here. I love you." She kissed Maci's temple. Why was it so easy to say to her friend and so hard to say to Lenka? How was she protecting herself by not saying it when she knew it was true?

Maci snaked an arm around Grace's waist and squeezed. "I guess I can't blame you for that when I just threatened to slap you silly if you were to break up with her."

"Exactly. You can't have it both ways."

Maci straightened. "It's almost May. How many more chances are there before June?"

"This one and then the one at the beginning of June." Grace's stomach churned with stress. It was always close these days, this stomach churning. She was happy with Lenka. Extremely happy. Being with her mostly kept the anxiety about losing her at bay. But it was there, waiting to mess with her stomach at any moment. This conversation was its opportunity.

But progress was being made in regards to Lenka staying. Not only all of her obsessive studying, but also, Memorial had found the money for a translator position and posted the job with Lenka in mind. The problem was twofold. One was that they had to advertise it and consider any qualified candidates who applied in a certain amount of time. If a US citizen applied and was equally or better qualified than Lenka, they would have to hire that person over her. Carissa had said that it was unlikely to happen, given that they'd put in several things that applied with fair uniqueness to Lenka, but it was possible.

The other was that the probable—or maybe only possible—job offer was contingent on Lenka being a fully qualified translator. That meant that she needed to pass this test in three languages—French, English, and Czech and between any of the three of them—in order to gain the qualification she needed.

She was working on it. And Grace was working extra to give her the time and space to do that. Lenka had gone into super study mode a couple of days ago and had a few days yet to go. Grace had been off two days ago, and she'd tried to be a support, but she could see that her offers of snacks, beverages, and meals were more intrusive than helpful. Lenka knew when it was the right time for a break. Grace showing up and breaking her concentration at inopportune times wasn't helpful. Also, after Lenka emerged from her room to find food one time, she'd ended up dragging Grace to bed. While she'd said it was a good stress relief in some ways, she'd also shown clear signs that she wasn't happy about the time away from her studies.

While Grace held the belief that breaks were good for concentration, Lenka's style was near-total submersion. Grace had used the rest of her day off to prepare easy-to-grab food and made herself available to pick up extra shifts until after Lenka's test.

"Okay, then, what does she need from us to pass?" Maci asked.

"Time alone to study." Grace stood and straightened her scrubs. "Which is why I'm here."

❖

Lenka looked up from her computer. "My eyes are blurring. Do you feel like a walk?"

Grace looked out the window, as was her habit when considering outdoor activities in spring. It wasn't currently raining. "Sure." She tucked her phone away.

Now that Lenka's test was over, she wasn't as immersed in studying. She'd seemed calmer now, too. Grace hoped that this calm meant that she felt good about how the test had gone. She'd been a little evasive when Grace had asked.

When they were ready and Grace opened the door, Loki shot out. "We're going out. You'll be stuck outside until we get back," she told him.

He stuck a leg in the air and cleaned himself unconcernedly.

"It's a nice day. I'm sure he'll be fine." Lenka had affection in her tone as she watched the little cat.

"I'm sure you're right. I just like to make sure he knows what he's getting into."

Lenka took her hand as they descended the stairs. "It's a good thought, but I'm not sure his English is that good."

"No? Do you speak cat now so you know for sure?"

Lenka gave a little shrug. "Of course."

Grace giggled. "You probably do. You speak all the languages."

"That is a bit of an exaggeration."

"Maybe, but you probably could if you wanted to."

They walked for a while, bantering and chatting about nothing, their steps taking them closer to Alberta.

"How would you feel about a coffee?" Lenka asked.

"Good. I'd feel good about a coffee." They were near Grace's favorite coffee shop. "Have you been here?"

Lenka laughed. "It was my very first find of the neighborhood."

Willa was behind the counter, as she seemed to be nearly every time Grace came in. She was still looking at a coworker she'd just said something to when she started to greet them, "What can I—" She looked fully at the two of them, surprise written all over her face. "You two. I didn't even know you knew each other, and you're together?" The end part shifted into a happy squeal.

Grace felt her cheeks heat. She'd always had a little bit of a flirtatious thing with Willa, but every customer who came in probably did.

"Yes," Lenka said with a twinkle in her eye. "Sorry, but she's mine."

Willa leaned over the counter and swatted Lenka on the shoulder. "I'd have taken either of you, to be honest. I can't believe that my two favorite customers are off the market."

"Oh, you're just saying that." Lenka was flirting with her, Grace realized.

She laughed. "Come sit with us if you've got time for a break, and we'll tell you the whole story."

They passed a very enjoyable half hour flirting with Willa while only having eyes for one another. It was really fun to tell their story to someone for whom it was brand-new, as well.

When they were walking back home, Grace said, "Do you think we really are her favorites, or does she flirt with everyone?"

"I suspect she flirts with everyone, but I also think she'd have been happy to date you. I saw the way she looked at you."

"Yeah, well, the only person I'm interested in dating is you." It was true, but it also made Grace's stomach hurt a little because she didn't know if she was going to get to keep dating Lenka after June. "Besides, I think you're the one everyone wants to date in this relationship."

Lenka scoffed.

Grace was flattered, but she knew Lenka was the catch. She just hoped she really had caught her and wasn't going to lose her.

❖

It was a Sunday, Grace was off, and she was spending it grocery shopping. It was a task that fell to her both because she was in charge of board as well as room—something that still made her feel a little squidgy when she thought about it—but also because she had more time. Lenka sometimes went with her, but today, she'd said she would stay home and get homework done so they could do something fun together later.

When Grace turned onto Holman, she noticed that her yard was full of people. Had something happened to Lenka? There were no flashing lights or anything to indicate an emergency, so probably not. As she drew closer, she realized she knew all these people. And they were doing yard work.

She parked and sat stunned for a moment, but everyone paused in their work and turned to her as she got out of the car.

"Surprise!"

Her gaze went from face to face, looking for some sort of explanation. When she landed on Lenka, she knew she'd found the person with the answers. She looked a little guilty, a little pleased. "I know you didn't know what to do about the yard, and it was stressing you out, so I organized a work party."

"Yeah," Maci said, "your girlfriend here guilted us all into this shit." She was smiling with a dirt streak on her cheek as she leaned on a shovel. She stood next to a pile of barkdust. There was another large pile in the driveway.

Greg was leaning on a rototiller in what looked like the last part of the yard to need tilling. Carissa was tacking down a large black sheet of something. Carson and Sue were kneeling over some plants. They weren't just doing a little yard work; they were landscaping the whole thing.

Grace felt tears well up. "You guys. This is amazing."

They all abandoned their tools and enveloped her in a group hug. "It's the least we could do for how often you feed us," Carson said.

"Okay, okay, enough swarming Grace," Lenka said. "Back to work."

Everyone went with good-natured grumbles, leaving Lenka and Grace alone. Lenka looked a little worried. "It's okay?"

Grace pulled her into a hug. "More than okay. You're amazing for doing this. I—" She couldn't say it. She just couldn't tell her. It would only make it worse if she had to leave. Not that everything she did didn't make it worse. She shook herself. "Let me get the groceries inside and change. Then I'll come help."

The rest of the afternoon was filled with hard work, but as they sat on the porch eating pizza and drinking beer afterward, Grace was filled with so many emotions that vied for attention. She loved her new yard. It was a thing of beauty that wouldn't require a lot of upkeep. Lenka had explained she'd done some research into native plants, and that was all that they'd used. But more than that, Grace felt such gratitude for her friends, such a sense of community. She loved all of them, but Lenka most of all.

"You probably passed." Grace squeezed Lenka's shoulders.

She was huddled into Grace, abnormally quiet. "You don't know that." She refreshed her email inbox, then set her phone aside for about the hundredth time. She'd taken the test two weeks prior and had been in good spirits until yesterday. Today was the day the results were due, and Grace had been aware she'd been awake much of the night tossing and turning.

"Not for sure." Grace squeezed again. "But you passed the practice test, so it's a good bet." She was reassuring herself as much as Lenka.

Lenka sat up and looked at her. "I hope so. I want to believe it. Honestly, I really, really want this because I want the hospital job, but what wrecks me is the possibility that I'll lose you because I can't pass some dumb test."

Grace took her hands. "You won't." She considered telling Lenka about her forays into exploring what it would take to move to Prague. She'd explored the options a few more times. There were English-speaking medical clinics in Prague who hired foreign nationals and sponsored visas. She could apply for one of those jobs. But as much as they'd both said they wanted a relationship, what if Lenka didn't really want Grace following her like some sad puppy dog? Maybe if Lenka had to move back, she'd want to forget this life altogether.

Besides, Grace wasn't completely sure she wanted to move to Prague, even if she could figure out all the visa issues. As much as she didn't want to lose Lenka, the thought of living in a whole other country was daunting, to say the least. She wasn't proficient in languages like Lenka was. And her friends were pillars in her life. Did she really want to move away from them? She did not. She needed to be super sure about the longevity of her and Lenka's relationship before she'd do anything like that. And they hadn't even said they loved each other yet. Maybe Lenka didn't. Maybe Grace was just convenient.

And it would be best for both of them if they could stay in Portland. This was home. And Lenka wanted to stay. Ugh. It was so hard.

She couldn't regret getting involved with Lenka, but these last couple of months had Grace feeling a more visceral understanding of what people with anxiety issues must have gone through. Of course it wasn't the same, but stress symptoms were never far away. Regardless of her own stress, what Lenka needed now was comfort. Their potential combined future was all on her shoulders.

She pulled Lenka into her for a hug. "You'll pass. If not this time, then next."

Lenka wrapped her arms around Grace and rested her head on Grace's shoulder. Then, she pulled back and looked at her phone again. "Oh my God. It's here."

Grace's shoulders clenched, but she pulled it together enough to put a comforting arm on Lenka's thigh.

"Okay, okay, okay. I'm going to open it. Ready?"

Grace nodded, but Lenka never looked up. She poked at her phone and, "I passed!" She stood and raised her fists in the air in triumph before vaulting onto the couch and jumping up and down.

Grace joined her. "You passed?"

"I passed."

"Congratulations, sweetheart. You're so awesome."

"I know." Lenka shimmied.

Grace laughed. If Lenka couldn't own it today of all days, then something was wrong with the world.

Lenka launched herself at Grace and kissed her into next week. Or at least out of her jeans.

They lay tangled together on the couch after and Lenka said, "Now I just need that job offer."

It turned out the stress was happy to come back into residence in Grace's belly.

❖

"What are you two going to do about the living situation after your exchange is officially up?" Maci wagged a finger between Grace and Lenka.

"Maci." Grace was mortified. They were having a dinner party at the end of May. There were nineteen days left on the original exchange student stay. Lenka was still waiting on a job offer. She'd broken down and applied to a handful of other places, and Grace supported her, but each job she'd applied to that wasn't in Portland was like its own little needle poke. Lenka had stopped telling her about them, so Grace supposed she hadn't hidden her anxiety that well.

In fact, they were communicating less about the future than when they'd first gotten together two months ago. Grace wanted to be with Lenka, and Lenka had said she wanted to be with Grace. But that was where they'd left it. Instead, they held each other while they watched movies and made fun of the plots. They made love to each other like there was no tomorrow. But they had stopped talking about the future.

While Grace had said that Lenka was welcome to continue to live here That Night, that had also been before they'd expressed feelings for each other. She didn't know if their relationship had changed how Lenka felt about living here. And now Maci was poking at that unknown. Worse, it was in front of their closest friends: Greg, Aubrey, Carissa, Carson, and Sue.

Maci's third glass of wine had loosened her tongue. Greg put a hand over hers. Grace hoped it was a suppressive hand. "What? It's a legit—"

"So," Aubrey said loudly, "what're your plans after graduation, Carson?"

Carson, Sue, and Lenka were all graduating from their programs next month. Grace hoped that Aubrey knew Carson had plans for after graduation because if not, that question was just as insensitive as Maci's.

Carson looked at ease, though. "I'm going to spend a year teaching English in Vietnam. I was inspired by Lenka."

Greg frowned. "I thought your major was literature or something."

She nodded. "It is. I am planning on graduate school eventually, but it turns out that you only need to have a bachelor's degree to teach English abroad with a lot of programs. So I'm doing that for a year. I'll go from there."

"And you're going back to China, right, Sue?" Carissa asked.

"Yes. I have a job lined up with a manufacturing firm that works internationally. They want me both for my programming and my English." Sue looked proud.

Grace was happy for both of them. And she hoped that she'd see them both again in the future. She'd enjoyed getting to know them. But she was also a little jealous that they had it figured out while Lenka was still in limbo.

Carissa shot Lenka a sympathetic look. "I'm sorry they still haven't officially offered."

Officially? What did that mean? Had there been an unofficial offer? If so, why hadn't Lenka told her. Grace shot her a questioning look.

Lenka shook her head subtly. “I went to talk to HR when I was at the hospital yesterday. They said it’s looking good, but they have to leave the notice up for five more days. It’s not new news.”

Grace digested that. It wasn’t exactly new news, but it was positive. If they’d said that they just had to see those five days out, then if no one else was qualified, Lenka was in, right? Five more days. She could make it five more days.

Carson said, “But none of those things happen if we don’t pass our classes, and finals aren’t until next week. We’re not done.”

Sue nodded solemnly. Lenka shrugged. “I mean, we’re not done, done, but it’d be hard for me to fail any classes now. Maybe if I just didn’t turn in my final papers. Even then, I think I’ve got the credits. And I’m done with my translating class back home. I just need to know about the job now.”

Many of those around the table murmured or gave her sympathetic looks. Maci, though, said, “Yeah, but if you do get the job, are you going to keep living here?”

Grace put her face in her hands.

CHAPTER TWENTY-NINE

Lenka popped into the volunteer office to drop off her time sheet for the previous week. She dropped it into the appropriate box and stuck her head into Carissa's office to say hi. Carissa was on the phone, so she waved and started to turn away, but Carissa held up a finger and indicated the spare chair.

Curious, Lenka sank onto the chair. Finals had been this week. She only had one week left as a volunteer. Then she would be… flying back to Prague? She had a ticket. It had been a requirement of her entry into the US, having a ticket back out. She'd paid scraped-together money for a fully refundable ticket because at the time, she'd hoped she'd be flying to New York for a shiny new job with the UN rather than back to Czechia. But she had the ticket and had yet to turn it in for the refund because she didn't know what was going to happen.

The five days HR had promised last week had passed with no offer. Maybe that meant that there had been another qualified candidate. Maybe a US citizen. No one had said it wasn't happening, but no one had given any positive signs, either. A couple of the places she'd applied to in other cities had gotten back to her, and she had interviews lined up, but if something didn't come through in the next week—

No. That was defeatist thinking. For one, she could leave the country, then reenter as a tourist and stay for up to three months while she continued to look for a job that would sponsor her work visa. She could just go to Canada for that. She was going to turn her ticket in. She needed that money. She just…hadn't yet.

If it hadn't been for Grace being there for her these last few months, Lenka didn't know how she'd have coped. On the other hand, if there were no Grace, Lenka would be less devastated if she couldn't stay, but the thought of life without Grace was like looking into a dark pit. Scary, unwelcoming, and no place Lenka wanted to explore.

There was no doubt that what she wanted was to be with Grace. The last two plus months had only proven that Lenka was right to have fallen in love with her. But all the uncertainty had been difficult on them both, and they'd been avoiding difficult discussions about the future because of all that uncertainty. Or at least, that was why Lenka had.

But she wanted to know what Grace was thinking about, well, everything. The question Maci had asked about where she'd live if she got to stay in Portland had been echoing around her head. Did it make sense for her and Grace to live together so soon? She should probably get her own place. Grace's look at the table had made Lenka think that might be what she wanted. It would be sensible. And yet, they'd been living together for ten months. Not together, together for all that time, certainly, but together both in a relationship sense and in a roommate sense for nearly three months. Lenka thought it had been going well, but she didn't want to move too fast.

She scoffed at her own thought. They'd gone from declaring interest to bed in a matter of minutes. Fast was long behind them.

There could be a lot of reasons why Grace hadn't brought it up. Maybe it *was* because Grace didn't want Lenka to live with her. It could be the future avoidance they'd both been guilty of. They hadn't spoken about afterward really at all, as if not talking about it meant not thinking about it. When they knew about where Lenka could or would be living, then they'd talk about their living situation.

Right?

Carissa finished her conversation, hung up, and smiled. "Hey."

"Hey." Lenka smiled back. It was genuine if weak. She really was happy to see Carissa, but the stress of not knowing was heavy on her shoulders.

Carissa gave her a sympathetic look. "This has been a rough bit for you. I'm sorry about that."

Lenka shrugged, trying for cavalier but sure she wasn't really pulling it off. "It's the life I chose wanting to immigrate, I guess."

"I guess. It seems like it should be easier to build a life with the woman you love." Carissa paused. "You do love her, right? You're not just—I don't know—looking for a marriage visa?"

Lenka was momentarily outraged, but she had to acknowledge that Carissa was only looking out for her friend. Also, she probably didn't know how challenging it was to get a marriage visa. The movies made it seem easy, but there were a lot of hoops to jump through and waiting periods, sometimes years. Then, she realized that Carissa had said love. Lenka didn't want to tell her before Grace, but she did love Grace, and she wanted to convince Carissa that her intentions were good. "No. I swear. I do love her, and I wouldn't marry someone I loved for a visa."

Carissa leaned forward looking excited. "You love her?"

"Yes. But don't tell her. I want her to hear it from me first."

"You haven't told her?"

Lenka winced. "No. I don't know if she feels the same, and I don't…we haven't…with everything being so…I'm waiting for the right time."

Carissa looked skeptical, but what she said was, "I guess."

Lenka didn't want to talk about that anymore. She smiled a half-smile, trying to broadcast that she was joking. She leaned forward and rested her forearms on the desk. "As for getting a visa of any sort, I'd consider marrying a friend. Just how mad would Aubrey be if you agreed to marry me?" She winked and sat back.

Carissa looked momentarily surprised, then laughed. "Aubrey thinks that marriage is a heterosexual capitalist construct, or so she claims. Sometimes I wonder if it's more a fear of commitment. Maybe if you and I announced our engagement, she'd come around."

Lenka laughed. "Well, then. There we go, a solution to both our problems." They smiled for a moment before Lenka felt the need to clarify. "But sadly, not really. Marriage visas are much harder than employment visas, all pop culture to the contrary."

"Really? That's wild. In that case, it's a good thing you're getting an employment visa."

It took a moment for Lenka to process those words. Or was Carissa still joking? "Are…" She swallowed and tried again. "Are you serious?"

Carissa's smile was huge. "I am. Duniway Memorial Hospital would like to formally offer you a position."

Lenka was magically on her feet and around Carissa's desk, hugging her. "You're serious. You're seriously serious?"

Carissa laughed and hugged her back. "I'm seriously serious. My buddy in HR told me I could tell you because we're friends. You'll have to go over there to get all the details and sign paperwork, but you're in."

"I'm in." Lenka pulled Carissa to her feet and jumped up and down, holding her hands until Carissa joined in.

"You're in."

"What's happening?" It was Aubrey, leaning against the doorjamb and looking at them bemusedly.

Lenka shot Carissa a look, trying to convey she should go with what Lenka was about to say. "Carissa has agreed to marry me for a visa."

Carissa put a hand over her mouth, and Lenka caught a flash of her smile before the look on Aubrey's face caught her full attention. She straightened and looked gobsmacked. Man, that was such a good word. Her mouth opened and closed like a fish out of water. She appeared to try to speak, only to get out a strangled noise. She cleared her throat. "I, um, what?"

"Yes. I couldn't ask Grace because what a mistake to marry someone you're dating. But Carissa here"—Lenka put an arm around her—"agreed. Isn't that great?"

Aubrey slumped against the door. "I…I mean, if that's…" She straightened again. "No."

"What do you mean?" Carissa asked sweetly. "You said marriage was bunk, so it shouldn't matter at all."

"You'd have to live together." Aubrey was the picture of affronted. "Prove a relationship. I don't want—Carissa, will you marry me?" Aubrey moved directly in front of them and went down on one knee. She looked up at Lenka. "No offense. I want you to stay in the country, but you can't marry my girl." She looked back at Carissa. "I want to marry you. If you'll accept."

Carissa had gone quite pale. "I—what?"

"Will you please agree to spend the rest of your life with me? It's what I want more than anything in the world." She looked completely sincere.

Lenka realized belatedly that she was the most awkward third wheel in the world, still standing there with her arm around Carissa. She carefully removed said arm and side-stepped away.

Carissa's hand shot out and grabbed her, holding her in place. "Lenka was joking. I just offered her the translator job on behalf of Memorial. We aren't—never were—getting married. It was a joke. You don't have to do this."

Aubrey looked between them. Lenka read embarrassment followed quickly by increased resolution. She took Carissa's hand. "Carissa Maire Mathews, I love you, and I want to spend the rest of my life with you. I'd be honored if you would agree to marry me."

Carissa dropped Lenka's arm. She took the opportunity to continue to scoot away. She took one last look at them as she exited the office. Carissa was nodding and crying. Lenka closed the door behind her.

That had taken a turn. A happy turn but a wild one. It was great. Lenka was seriously happy for them both. But even more so, she was excited to tell Grace. First, she needed to make sure it was real, and there were no surprises. She couldn't imagine Carissa playing such an elaborate and mean practical joke, but she wouldn't quite believe it until she signed the paperwork. She set off for HR. The only thing keeping her from running was the hospital safety rules. She'd do nothing to jeopardize her chances.

When the HR visit proved Carissa was as good as her word, Lenka signed the contract, agreeing to start work in just one week. It was amazing how the gears could turn so slowly and suddenly be in overdrive. They'd filed paperwork for Lenka's visa, and all Lenka needed to do there was bring in her passport. She'd have a temporary visa to start with while the long-term one was acquired, but she was assured that they were used to dealing with these things and would get it done.

Lenka left and walked to the emergency room at just under a run. She hoped Grace wasn't with a patient. She used her badge to enter the ward and had a flash of the first time she'd come into this area with her broken arm, barely taking everything in. Now she'd been here dozens of times to visit Grace or translate for a patient. Then, it had been scary and unknown. Now, it was familiar and welcome, if only because she knew she'd find Grace here.

Only when she came rushing in, there was no Grace. It was Maci and a doctor, both of whom looked at her with alarm.

Lenka held her hands up. "No emergency. Everything is fine."

Maci exchanged a look with the doctor, who scowled and went back to whatever he was doing on the computer. Maci narrowed her eyes in a playful scowl. "Give us a heart attack, why don't you?"

Lenka went to lean on the counter. "You'd be in the right place for one, no?"

"Doesn't mean I want to have one. The heart attack part isn't so horrible if it doesn't kill you, but the aftereffects? Pretty bad. Surgery, long recovery. It's a mess. No, thank you. If not a heart attack of your own or another broken arm, what brings you rushing into the ED today?" Maci looked around as if to check to see if someone was waiting. "Did someone call you for translating?"

"No." Lenka grinned, thinking about her news. "I wanted to tell Grace some exciting news."

"Oh my God. You got the job, didn't you?"

Lenka patted the air in a shushing motion. She didn't want Grace to hear it from anyone other than her. She leaned in even closer. "Yes."

Maci leaned on the desk. "Why are we whispering?"

"Because I don't want Grace to hear."

"Hear what?"

Lenka jumped and spun around. "You're here!"

"Yes. I do work here." Grace smiled a crooked little smile. "I was scheduled for a shift. All of that makes this not a good place to talk about things you want to keep secret from me."

"I don't really want to keep it a secret. I just wanted you to hear it from me first." Lenka looked down and shook her head. "I'm messing this up."

When she looked back up, Grace was frowning. "Is something wrong?"

Lenka slapped a hand to her forehead. "No. The opposite. Okay, I'm just going to say it. I got the job."

Grace's face was slack for just a moment before it lit up. "The job here at Memorial? Are you serious? You got the job?" By the end, she was nearly yelling.

"I did." Lenka matched her energy. "I'm staying."

Grace cupped her cheeks and pulled her in for a scorching kiss. Lenka melted into her. She was staying. She was going to get to keep her life here in Portland, the life with her friends, a job she loved, and Grace. She kissed her back with all the relief and excitement that was coursing through her.

Someone cleared their throat. Grace smiled against her lips. "I guess we have an audience."

Lenka looked across the desk to see that Maci was standing with her hands clasped under her chin, looking delighted. The doctor was the one looking disapproving. Lenka kissed Grace one more time, then scooted back. Only then did she see that several patients were watching from their rooms, as well as an orderly and another nurse. Most looked amused.

Lenka refused to feel embarrassed, but she also opted not to go in for another kiss.

Maci came around the desk and hugged them both. "I'm so happy for you two."

Another nurse clapped Grace on the shoulder. "I see you've gotten some good news, which is great, but you're up for the next patient, and their room is ready. Back to work."

Grace pulled Lenka into a hug and whispered in her ear: "We'll celebrate when I get off work, okay?"

Lenka put her mouth right next to Grace's ear and said as softly as she could manage, "We're going to celebrate until neither of us can walk."

Grace moaned a little bit. "You're going to get me in trouble."

It was all Lenka could do not to drag her into a closet or something. Weren't doctors and nurses always going off into empty patient rooms for quickies? Only it couldn't have been in a hospital like Duniway, or at least, not the Duniway emergency room. The only thing separating these rooms from the hallway surrounding the nursing station was curtains. So instead of dragging Grace off, she released her with a look that she hoped conveyed her very real intentions to follow through with what she'd said.

As she was walking out, Aubrey walked in looking like she wasn't very clear on where she was or why. So many gobsmacked people today.

"Congratulations, Aubrey," Lenka said.

"Oh, yeah." Aubrey straightened. "Thanks. I…I think I'm getting married."

"What?" Maci was passing just behind Lenka. "What is going on today? Guys," she called out to the floor, "in addition to Lenka's new job, Aubrey and Carissa are getting married." Softer, she said, "It is Carissa you're marrying, right?"

Aubrey looked amused by this turn of events. "Of course. Holy shit. I'm getting married."

There was another scrum of hugs and congratulations, but it didn't last long before the charge nurse was there, breaking things up and sending people back to work.

Lenka went home to tell the person she was second most excited to tell the news. It was midnight in France, but Lenka was going to call her grand-mere.

When Grand-mere answered the phone, she was wearing a casual look: a silky cream shirt covered by a light black jacket. Earrings dangled from her lobes. Lenka was pretty sure she wouldn't have woken her, but the sight of her dressed for an evening out relieved any last doubt.

"Lenka, my little cabbage," Grand-mere said in French. "How are you?"

"Good, great, even." Lenka realized she'd started in English. Of her three languages, it was the one she used to default to the least, so it came as something of a surprise, although it probably shouldn't have been. She had been speaking it primarily for nearly a year now. She switched to French. "I got the job, Grand-mere."

Grand-mere clasped her hands to her chest. "That is wonderful. I'm so happy for you. What does your Grace say about this?"

Lenka basked under her gaze. "She was so happy. We only got to talk for a few minutes because she was at work, but she's very happy, too." Her mood shifted to serious. They'd have to have the living arrangement talk. Lenka was fine with moving. She didn't want to assume she was welcome in Grace's home past her exchange period. But it was so close now, and there wasn't much time to find another place. She would do it, of course, but in addition to finding a place, there was the actual move, figuring out furnishing, and… and leaving Grace. She didn't want to. But she didn't know if Grace was in the same place.

"What has happened? What are you thinking about?"

Lenka explained her thoughts.

"Well, my little cabbage, that is something you will need to discuss with her. But it will work out. These things always do."

She was right. Look at how the job had come through. Things would work out. Meanwhile, all she wanted to think about was how to celebrate. Today, that was all about being with Grace, but soon, there would also have to be a dinner party. They would have to celebrate Carissa and Aubrey's engagement, too. She discussed menu options with Grand-mere, which led to her telling Lenka about her evening at a friend's house.

Eventually, while Grand-mere still seemed quite present, Lenka felt bad about keeping her up so late and ended the call.

She went to the kitchen and got to work. By the time Grace was home hours later, she had an expansive spread laid out for them.

Grace, however, had different priorities. When Lenka went to the living room to greet her, Grace finished toeing off her second shoe, then flew across the room to sweep Lenka into a hug that turned into a kiss that meant they ended up down the hall in Lenka's room for quite a while before Grace said, "I feel like I interrupted plans. Something smells wonderful."

Lenka kissed her. "No interruption. This is the real plan. But I did spend the afternoon cooking. All stuff that would hold. I suspected something like this might happen."

"That was some seriously good planning. We should go check it out, I think."

"To the kitchen."

They pulled on T-shirts, Grace ending up in one of Lenka's. Lenka was a lot smaller, but she had some oversized shirts that worked on Grace. She liked seeing Grace in her shirt, not only for the usual couple reasons but also because it was a little snug on her. She enjoyed the display of Grace's curves.

In the kitchen, Grace picked up a flatbread studded with olives and onions. She ripped a piece off and took a bite. Lenka watched, still more interested in her than food.

Grace moaned. "This is so good. Is this the same recipe you made at the last dinner party? That was good, but this is better. Or am I just starving?"

"It might be both. I tweaked the recipe a little."

Grace popped another piece in her mouth. "It's a good tweak."

Lenka went for some water before tackling the food. Grace joined her at the sink, pressing her side to Lenka's.

"If you keep that up, I won't let you finish eating before I drag you back to bed." She was lying, though. Grace had worked all day and needed to eat.

"I'm not sure that would exactly be a tragedy." Grace drank long and deep, then wiped her mouth with the back of her hand.

Lenka watched every move, her own water forgotten.

"Drink up," Grace prompted. "We don't want you dehydrated."

Lenka drank. Slaking her thirst woke her appetite, but she still just looked at the roasted veggies she was standing next to. Having torn her gaze away from Grace, her brain was working overtime. She was staying, but what did that mean for her and Grace? Was now the time to tell Grace she loved her, or would that feel like pressure to let her stay here rather than finding her own place?

She was still staring at the food when Grace ran her hand down her back. "Is something wrong? Do you…are you sad about not going home?"

"No!" Grace looked surprised at her vehemence. She softened her tone. "No. I'm not sad. I'm so happy. I just…"

Grace put a finger under her chin. "You just what? You can tell me."

Lenka took a shaky breath. "I love you. I don't mean to tell you to pressure you or anything, but I love you, and I wanted you to know."

Grace seemed a mixture of surprised, pleased, and confused. "I…what?"

"I love you. I'm sorry."

"No, I got that part. The *I love you* part, which is great because I love you, too, but what is the pressure part, and why are you sorry?"

"You love me?" Lenka's heart pounded in her chest.

Grace smiled a slow smile. "I do. Didn't you know?"

"I hoped, but I wasn't sure. You hadn't said."

"Well, neither had you."

"But now we have."

"Yes." Grace pulled her in for a kiss. "We have. Now. Clear up the other part."

"What other part?" Lenka was hazy from the kiss and from the joy of knowing that Grace loved her. She was wrapped in Grace's arms, feeling like she'd come home.

"The pressure and the sorry part."

"Oh, that."

"Yes, that."

“I, um, didn’t want you to feel pressure to let me keep living here. I thought if I told you I loved you, you might think it was just to—I don’t know—have a place to live.”

“Do you not want to live here anymore?”

“I, well, I don’t want…”

“It’s okay if you don’t want to. I get it. There’s no pressure. But, Lenka?”

Lenka pulled back a little so she could look up. “Yes?”

“I would like you to, if you want to. I don’t want you to leave.”

Lenka felt her face curve into a smile of its own accord. “Really?”

“Really. I love you, and I want to live with you. If that’s what you want.”

With each word Grace said, Lenka’s heart grew until she got to the if. There was a slight hint of uncertainty in Grace’s voice that Lenka hurried to erase. “It’s what I want most in the world.”

Chapter Thirty

Grace felt like she could fly. Lenka was staying in Portland. She loved Grace, and she was going to continue to live with her. All her stress of the last couple of months finally melted away. She could climb mountains with the elation she felt.

Instead, she pushed the tray of roasted vegetables to the side and lifted Lenka onto the counter.

"I love you," Grace said less than an inch away from Lenka's mouth. The fact that she could say it freely sent a jolt of pleasure though her.

"I love you, too, kotě."

Grace had wanted to hear those words so much and to know that this relationship wasn't going to be a brief fling. She rested her forehead against Lenka's. "You came into my life and took me completely by surprise."

Lenka laughed. "I remember."

"But," Grace pushed on, "the initial surprise turned into the surprise of loving you. I couldn't admit it even to myself because I thought you were going to leave, but when you said you were staying…I had no willpower to resist you any longer. But I thought that if I kept the love declarations out of it, it wouldn't hurt so much if you had to leave. Then, I realized that saying it or not didn't matter. It would have broken me to have you walk out of my life. That's when I looked into what I'd have to do to get a visa for living in the Czech Republic."

Lenka's arms tightened around her. "You did?" She sounded amazed.

"I did. It was scary, but I thought, if you couldn't stay, maybe I'd have to go, too."

"Grace."

Then, her mouth was on Grace's, and all Grace could do was kiss her back. Their kiss was soft, nearly tentative at first. It was their first after their declared love. While having told one another how they really felt made Grace feel more secure in their relationship, it also felt new and precious with those words having been said. She tried to put all of that into their kiss.

The kiss grew from soft and sweet to deep and hungry. Grace put her hands under Lenka's shirt and smoothed them up her sides. She felt so good under Grace's hands. Her skin was soft and warm. She could feel the pace of Lenka's breathing pick up, her ribs expanding and contracting. She cradled one of Lenka's breasts, and her breathing stopped before picking back up.

Lenka tugged on Grace's shirt—well, Lenka's shirt—and Grace answered by removing Lenka's shirt first, then allowing Lenka to remove hers. This would, remarkable considering the last few months, be the christening of the kitchen, but it was actually a good room in terms of privacy.

When Lenka took Grace's nipple into her mouth, all thoughts fled. Grace cupped the back of Lenka's head and arched into her. Lenka took more of her breast into her mouth, and Grace moaned her approval. If she'd been wearing panties, they'd have been soaked. She moved her hips, searching for pressure, and Lenka took the hint, moving a hand to Grace's center.

"Wait," Grace gasped out.

Lenka froze. "Is something wrong?"

"Nothing at all. I just…want this to be slow."

Lenka nodded. "Yes."

Grace kissed her, resuming her exploration of Lenka's form. She wanted to touch her everywhere, and she did. From her hands in Lenka's hair to kissing up the inside of Lenka's legs, Grace worshiped her. By the time she put her mouth over Lenka's center, Lenka was whimpering.

"Grace." Lenka's hands were in Grace's hair. She pulled a little, which nearly caused Grace to come undone even with that being Lenka's only hold on her. She sucked Lenka's clit in response. "Grace," Lenka repeated, sounding like she was having difficulty forming words. She pulled harder. "Come up here. I want to look at you."

Grace gave her center one last kiss, then complied. She wanted the same. She brushed her thumb's over Lenka's cheeks as she pressed their bodies together. "I love you."

"I love you." Lenka slid a hand between them and cupped her.

Grace moved against her hand involuntarily. Her breathing quickened. She slid two fingers into Lenka's wet folds, then, knowing she was ready, pushed those fingers inside. Lenka gasped.

It was a matter of a few moments before Grace felt herself tipping over the edge. She forced her eyes to stay open and focused on Lenka.

"I'm, Grace, I'm—" Lenka clamped around her fingers, and that was it. Pleasure ripped through her as she watched Lenka shatter.

They slumped together, supporting each other. Grace enjoyed this after time, good feelings coursing through her still, love for Lenka surging again until she felt the need to tell her about it. "I love you." She was resting her head on Lenka's shoulder, face nestled in her neck, close enough that her lips moved against Lenka's skin.

Lenka's hand smoothed up her back to her neck. "I could hear that every day, and it would never get old."

"Good because that's my plan."

Epilogue

Six Months Later

Lenka took Grace's hand. "You were very brave, kotě."

Grace laughed. "Please. It was just a plane flight. Thousands of people do it every day."

"It wasn't just a flight. It was your first ever plane travel and to another country. You had to get a passport and travel for eighteen hours."

Grace pulled her phone out of her bag. "Only sixteen hours, so far. I think. If I'm doing the time change correctly."

Lenka kissed her cheek. "You're adorable. And correct. It'll take us time to get the bags and take the train to Grand-mere's. But the hard part is done. Your first two flights are behind you, and you cleared passport control."

"It wasn't exactly challenging."

"I know, but you did it by yourself." Because they had passports from different countries, they'd gone separately. For all that Grace was cavalier about it now, Lenka had gone over what to expect a couple of times beforehand.

Grace huffed. "Baby's first passport control."

Lenka squeezed her hand. "Everyone has to have a first time. Unless they don't leave their country, I guess."

"If I'd never met you, that very well might have been me. Oh, there's your bag, I think."

It was. Lenka was traveling with the luggage she'd purchased for the exchange, a bag that had been on clearance likely because no one else wanted to buy the thing. It was hard-sided, bright blue, and had colorful mock tickets on it. She grabbed it off the conveyer belt. "Now we just need yours."

They waited, tired but chatting happily about their trip until the conveyer stopped turning. Grace's bag never showed.

"What do we do now?" Grace asked.

"They'll send it on. We just need to go tell the baggage people about it. I'm sorry this happened on your first trip." Lenka looked around for their airline's baggage office, found it, and pointed it out. They walked over.

"Oh well," Grace said. "At least I'm traveling with a pro so I knew to cross pack."

Lenka buffed her fingernails. "I've got you covered, kotě."

Grace put an arm around her. "I know. Same."

"I know."

Grace had helped her so much through the adjustment period. Lenka had thought it would be seamless to go from being a student to working and living long-term in the US. She'd already been doing the same job, and not having schoolwork should have made things easier. And it did, but Lenka actually missed school. She was considering going back for another degree, maybe in literature or gender studies.

But the politics of working at the hospital had shifted with the change from volunteer to paid employee. It was all fine, but it had been a surprise. It wasn't just Grace who'd helped out there but their whole friend group. However, the very reason Lenka had those friends was because of Grace. And now, they made up nearly her entire friend group. Her friends from last year had scattered either back to their home countries or were off on new adventures.

But work was the least of it. Now that Lenka was in the US for good, she needed things like a driver's license. Navigating the DMV was no joke, but Grace had been by her side, supporting her through the three visits it took to finally have the right paperwork.

Grace had been the one in a position to lend support and guidance in their relationship so far. Now, it was Lenka's turn. She didn't mind either role, but having some of each was a plus. To be fair, it was already starting to smooth out at home as Lenka found her footing.

They took care of the bag situation, leaving Grand-mere's address for delivery when the bag finally showed, and exited the airport.

"To the train station," Lenka said, leading the way to the transit stop. She had been flying into Paris to visit Grand-mere since she was a little girl. By the time she was a teenager, Grand-mere no longer came all the way to the airport to meet her but let her navigate her way to the small town to the southeast.

"Wait." Grace put a hand on Lenka's arm. She pointed with her other. "Isn't that—"

"Grand-mere!" Lenka rushed over and hugged her. "What are you doing here?"

"It's a special occasion, meeting your partner," she said in strongly accented English for Grace's sake. She hugged Lenka back and turned her attention to Grace. "Welcome to France."

Grace beamed. She and Grand-mere had video chatted and were already extremely fond of one another. Grand-mere opened her arms to Grace, who stepped right into the embrace with no hesitation. "It's so good to finally meet you in person," Grace said.

Grand-mere squeezed her arm and smiled at her. "I'm so glad to meet you in person, as well, the woman who is making my Lenka so happy."

Grace turned her smile on Lenka, who smiled back, unashamed.

"Come now." Grand-mere looked down. "Did you only bring one suitcase between you? Traveling light, a good motto," she continued before either of them answered. "Louis?"

Only when a man stepped forward did Lenka realize that he was with Grand-mere. It made sense, as Grand-mere didn't drive. She didn't even own a car. She said that walking everywhere, which was very doable in her small town, was good for her health. If she was going farther, she said she preferred the train. The fact she'd gotten a driver for them was a big deal.

Louis, at Grand-mere's direction, took the bag and led them to the car at the curb. He opened the door at the back for them and loaded the bag into the trunk.

"Fancy, Grand-mere," Lenka said. "And there is another bag coming. It didn't make the connection."

"Airlines," Grand-mere said dismissively. "And of course, only the best for my granddaughters."

Grace looked surprised at the plural at first, but she shot Lenka a knowing smile. It was clear she thought it was a mistake from a nonnative speaker. Grand-mere reached across Lenka to pat Grace's knee. "You're one of mine, now."

Grace smiled a pleased, slightly embarrassed sort of smile. Lenka threaded their fingers together. She knew how much it meant to Grace, who'd had such a close relationship with her grandma, to have a grandmother in her life once more.

Louis navigated out of the airport, and the next thing Lenka knew, she was waking up as the car parked in Grand-mere's driveway.

❖

Grace was woken from a dream involving introducing Lenka to her grandma by a gentle shoulder shake.

"We're here," Lenka said.

"Oh, sorry. I didn't mean to fall asleep." She rubbed her eyes and stretched.

Lenka's grand-mere was already out of the car, but she stuck her head back in. "Do not worry, you were not the only one. Louis and I had a lovely chat on the way home. Do come in. We'll have a light lunch, and then you two can nap again if you need to."

"We should push through until bedtime. It'll help us adjust," Lenka said.

That made sense. Grace had been amazed by Lenka on the trip. She was confident and capable, which were very sexy qualities. It reminded Grace of each of the first times she'd realized Lenka's faculty with various languages. She should maybe avoid a nap, but she could think of other reasons to retreat to a bedroom.

Grace got out of the car and saw Grand-mere waiting for them. Or maybe not. She would have felt awkward about having sex under her grandma's roof. Maybe Lenka would feel the same.

Louis was already at the door with Lenka's suitcase, which drew her attention to the house. Grand-mere's house had been described to her as a cottage, but it didn't look like any cottage Grace was familiar with. The car was parked on a drive that was surrounded on three sides by the house. The door was in the middle. Grace knew little to nothing about architecture, so she didn't know the names of the features she was seeing, but the roof slanted up to meet in a ridge along the top. Things—chimneys, maybe, although there were at least two—jutted out of the flat part on the top. The center part of the house had stone walls, but the rest was stucco.

There appeared to be an upstairs. The roof was tall enough, and there was a window up there. Aside from the two large windows framing the front door, all the windows had wooden shutters. The whole thing was at least twice the size of Grace's house. And it was decorated for Christmas as if a decorator for some upscale country living magazine had personally created a look for it.

In a word, it was stunning.

"Wow."

"Yeah, Grand-mere goes all out for Christmas."

That wasn't all that Grace had thought, but it was close enough. Lenka took her hand to lead her to the door. She pointed up. "That's my room, our room. It's a sweet little attic room. Grand-mere has offered different rooms over the years, but it's my favorite." With more volume, she said, "That's right, Grand-mere, isn't it? We'll be staying in the attic room."

"Of course, my little cabbage."

The house was just as lovely inside. Lenka led her excitedly on a tour culminating in the attic room, which was, indeed, sweet. The double bed was at one end under a window and had sloping walls on either side, meaning that one either had to crawl onto the bed from the foot of it or hunch over to approach.

Grace flopped down face-first. “Why am I so tired?” Her voice came out muffled by the duvet.

“Because it’s about three a.m. back home, and you’ve been up for about twenty hours now?”

The mattress dipped on one side, and Lenka’s hand rubbed little circles on her back.

It was dark when Grace woke up. Shoot. She’d fallen asleep when she was supposed to have stayed up until bedtime to adjust. She was farther up the bed than where she’d fallen. She must have scooted up because there was no way that Lenka could have hauled her up. But also, her shoes were off, and there was a blanket on her. That was certainly Lenka’s work. As always, that consideration made her feel warm and cared for. Lenka was sleeping next to her but under the covers.

Grace resisted the urge to touch her, not wanting to wake her. Instead, she quietly slipped out of bed and went to the bathroom where, in addition to relieving herself, she washed her face. She went back into their bedroom and undressed before climbing back onto the bed under the covers.

Lenka shifted and mumbled. Grace wasn’t sure if she was awake or not. “Go back to sleep, sweetheart. I’m sorry I woke you.”

Lenka rolled over and opened her eyes. “You’re awake.”

“Yeah. Sorry I fell asleep again.”

Lenka smoothed her hair. “Don’t worry about it. You clearly needed it. Do you think you can go back to sleep?”

“Probably.” Grace kissed Lenka’s neck. “Unless you had something else in mind.”

They made quiet, sleepy love under the covers. Grace was happy to have the connection and fall back asleep with Lenka in her arms.

The next morning was Christmas Eve. When Grace woke, Lenka was gone. Grace figured she was downstairs with Grand-mere. She lay in bed for a few minutes while she woke up and felt a small pang about not being at home to host her usual friends’ dinner, but they’d be back next year. This year, she was in France. And she had a plan.

With that thought, she was too excited to stay in bed any longer. She tossed the covers back and rummaged in Lenka's bag for her cross packed outfit. After a shower, she pulled on the jeans and sweater and went downstairs.

There were morning greetings, Christmas Eve greetings, croissants, and coffee. The kiss from Lenka made the morning perfect. When Lenka left the room, Grace quickly checked in with Grand-mere to make sure the plan was still on.

"Yes, of course." Grand-mere looked at the clock. "We'll go in an hour, which should be perfect timing."

She patted Grace's hand, then produced a box. Grace's stomach lurched with recognition and excitement. She took the box and with trembling fingers, opened it. It was just as lovely as she'd imagined. She closed it and tucked it away before Lenka could return.

She put her hand over Grand-mere's, feeling brave. "Thank you. This means the world to me, and I know it'll mean everything to Lenka."

Grand-mere's eyes sparkled. "I wish you both all the happiness."

Lenka came back and eyed them curiously. Grace innocently picked up her coffee and took a sip. Her stomach twinged with a hint of stress reminiscent of the stress of spring, but now, it was mostly with excitement. A little bit of nerves was normal for a plan of this magnitude. It was fine.

When the time came, they all bundled up and walked to the town square. As Grand-mere had promised, a choir was singing Christmas carols in front of the tree. There were booths set up selling warm things to eat and drink. It smelled wonderful, but Grace ignored them for now.

Some of her nerves must have shown because Lenka looked at her with concern. "Are you okay?"

There was no time like the present. Grace sank down on one knee. Lenka's eyes went wide, and her hand went to her mouth.

"You told me that it was last Christmas Eve when you realized that I made you feel like you were home. Sweetheart, you've been my home for at least that long. I'd like nothing more than to be each other's home forever. Lenka Draha Supik, will you marry me?"

Grace presented the box. It contained Grand-mere's own wedding ring, resized to fit Lenka.

"I will." Lenka pulled on her hands. "Oh my God, get up here so I can kiss you."

When Grace got to her feet, Lenka threw her arms around her shoulders, pulling her in for a kiss. When they parted, several people around them clapped.

Grace beamed. "Let me put the ring on."

Lenka held her hand up to admire the ring, and her eyes got shiny. "Grand-mere, this is…thank you."

Grand-mere looked at both of them with love and affection. "You will make beautiful brides."

Grace slipped the ring on and felt like everything in her life was clicking into place. "I'm so glad I couldn't find a roommate last year," she said inanely.

Lenka got it, though because they understood each other. "Me too, kotě."

About the Author

Sage is a board game enthusiast and occasional hiker who enjoys reading and writing books about women. When the weather allows, she's further distracted by her stand up paddle board.

She always makes time to snuggle with her beloved dog and chat excitedly about books with her daughter. Sage lives in Portland, Oregon.

Books Available from Bold Strokes Books

Language Lessons by Sage Donnell. Grace and Lenka never expected to fall in love. Is home really where the heart is if it means giving up your dreams? (978-1-63679-725-0)

New Horizons by Shia Woods. When Quinn Collins meets Alex Anders, Horizon Theater's enigmatic managing director, a passionate connection ignites, but amidst the complex backdrop of theater politics, their budding romance faces a formidable challenge. (978-1-63679-683-3)

Scrambled: A Tuesday Night Book Club Mystery by Jaime Maddox. Avery Hutchins makes a discovery about her father's death that will force her to face an impossible choice between doing what is right and finally finding a way to regain a part of herself she had lost. (978-1-63679-703-8)

Stolen Hearts by Michele Castleman. Finding the thief who stole a precious heirloom will become Ella's first move in a dangerous game of wits that exposes family secrets and could lead to her family's financial ruin. (978-1-63679-733-5)

Synchronicity by J.J. Hale. Dance, destiny, and undeniable passion collide at a summer camp as Haley and Cal navigate a love story that intertwines past scars with present desires. (978-1-63679-677-2)

The First Kiss by Patricia Evans. As the intrigue surrounding her latest case spins dangerously out of control, military police detective Parker Haven must choose between her career and the woman she's falling in love with. (978-1-63679-775-5)

Wild Fire by Radclyffe & Julie Cannon. When Olivia returns to the Red Sky Ranch, Riley's carefully crafted safe world goes up in flames. Can they take a risk and cross the fire line to find love? (978-1-63679-727-4)

Writ of Love by Cassidy Crane. Kelly and Jillian struggle to navigate the ruthless battleground of Big Law, grappling with desire, ambition, and the thin line between success and surrender. (978-1-63679-738-0)

Back to Belfast by Emma L. McGeown. Two colleagues are asked to trade jobs. Claire moves to Vancouver and Stacie moves to Belfast, and though they've never met in person, they can't seem to escape a growing attraction from afar. (978-1-63679-731-1)

Exposure by Nicole Disney and Kimberly Cooper Griffin. For photographer Jax Bailey and delivery driver Trace Logan, keeping it casual is a matter of perspective. (978-1-63679-697-0)

Hunt of Her Own by Elena Abbott. Finding forever won't be easy, but together Danaan's and Ashly's paths lead back to the supernatural sanctuary of Terabend. (978-1-63679-685-7)

Perfect by Kris Bryant. They say opposites attract, but Alix and Marianna have totally different dreams. No Hollywood love story is perfect, right? (978-1-63679-601-7)

Royal Expectations by Jenny Frame. When childhood sweethearts Princess Teddy Buckingham and Summer Fisher reunite, their feelings resurface and so does the public scrutiny that tore them apart. (978-1-63679-591-1)

Shadow Rider by Gina L. Dartt. In the Shadows, one can easily find death, but can Shay and Keagan find love as they fight to save the Five Nations? (978-1-63679-691-8)

The Breakdown by Ronica Black. Vaughn and Natalie have chemistry, but the outside world keeps knocking at the door, threatening more trouble, making the love and the life they want together impossible. (978-1-63679-675-8)

Tribute by L.M. Rose. To save her people, Fiona will be the tribute in a treaty marriage to the Tipruii princess, Simaala, and spend the rest of her days on the other side of the wall between their races. (978-1-63679-693-2)

Wild Wales by Patricia Evans. When Finn and Aisling fall in love, they must decide whether to return to the safety of the lives they had, or take a chance on wild love in windswept Wales. (978-1-63679-771-7)

Can't Buy Me Love by Georgia Beers. London and Kayla are perfect for one another, but if London reveals she's in a fake relationship with Kayla's ex, she risks not only the opportunity of her career, but Kayla's trust as well. (978-1-63679-665-9)

Chance Encounter by Renee Roman. Little did Sky Roberts know when she bought the raffle ticket for charity that she would also be taking a chance on love with the egotistical Drew Mitchell. (978-1-63679-619-2)

Comes in Waves by Ana Hartnett. For Tanya Brees, love in small-town Coral Bay comes in waves, but can she make it stay for good this time? (978-1-63679-597-3)

Dancing With Dahlia by Julia Underwood. How is Piper Fernley supposed to survive six weeks with the most controlling, uptight boss on earth? Because sometimes when you stop looking, your heart finds exactly what it needs. (978-1-63679-663-5)

Skyscraper by Gun Brooke. Attempting to save the life of an injured boy brings Rayne and Kaelyn together. As they strive for justice against corrupt Celestial authorities, they're unable to foresee how intertwined their fates will become. (978-1-63679-657-4)

The Curse by Alexandra Riley. Can Diana Dillon and her daughter, Ryder, survive the cursed farm with the help of Deputy Mel Defoe? Or will the land choose them to be the next victims? (978-1-63679-611-6)

The Heart Wants by Krystina Rivers. Fifteen years after they first meet, Army Major Reagan Jennings realizes she has one last chance to win the heart of the woman she's always loved. If only she can make Sydney see she's worth risking everything for. (978-1-63679-595-9)

Untethered by Shelley Thrasher. Helen Rogers, in her eighties, meets much-younger Grace on a lengthy cruise to Bali, and their intense relationship yields surprising insights and unexpected growth. (978-1-63679-636-9)

You Can't Go Home Again by Jeanette Bears. After their military career ends abruptly, Raegan Holcolm is forced back to their hometown to confront their past and discover where the road to recovery will lead them, or if it already led them home. (978-1-636790644-4)

A Wolf in Stone by Jane Fletcher. Though Cassilania is an experienced player in the dirty, dangerous game of imperial Kavillian politics, even she is caught out when a murderer raises the stakes. (978-1-63679-640-6)

One Last Summer by Kristin Keppler. Emerson Fields didn't think anything could keep her from her dream of interning at Bardot Design Studio in Paris, until an unexpected choice at a North Carolina beach has her questioning what it is she really wants. (978-1-63679-638-3)

StreamLine by Lauren Melissa Ellzey. When Lune crosses paths with the legendary girl gamer Nocht, she may have found the key that will boost her to the upper echelon of streamers and unravel all Lune thought she knew about gaming, friendship, and love. (978-1-63679-655-0)

The Devil You Know by Ali Vali. As threats come at the Casey family from both the feds and enemies set to destroy them, Cain Casey does whatever is necessary with Emma at her side to bury every single one. (978-1-63679-471-6)

The Meaning of Liberty by Sage Donnell. When TJ and Bailey get caught in the political crossfire of the ultraconservative Crusade of the Redeemer Church, escape is the only plan. On the run and fighting for their lives is not the time to be falling for each other. (978-1-63679-624-6)

Undercurrent by Patricia Evans. Can Tala and Wilder catch a serial killer in Salem before another body washes up on the shore? (978-1-636790669-7)

Bold Strokes Books
Quality and Diversity in LGBTQ Literature